That's the Life Baby

That's the Life Baby

An Idiot's Love Story

.....Thodi masti,
thoda pyar,
baaki sab bakwas.....

A novel by

Priyesh Ranjan

MP
MAHAVEER PUBLISHERS

Published by
MAHAVEER PUBLISHERS
4764/2A, 23-Ansari Road, Daryaganj
New Delhi - 110002
Ph. : 011 - 66629669-79-89
Fax : 011 - 41563419
e-mail : mahaveerpublishers@gmail.com

First Published 2010
Second Impression 2010

That's the Life Baby
ISBN (10) : 8183520006
ISBN (13) : 9788183520003

Distributed by
VAIBHAV BOOK SERVICE
e-mail : vaibhavbookservice@gmail.com

Published by D.K. Jha for Mahaveer Publishers
Printed by Jaico Printers, New Delhi

Dedicated to

Papa & Maa

Acknowledgement

This book could not have been possible without the two years of my stay at Kota. You learn more from life when you are away from home. The good part about writing this book was that I fell in love with my characters. My obsession with them remains everlasting.

I am thankful to my college friends—Anuj, Pranav, Sanchit, Akshay, Jay, Anand, Sudhanshu, Yogesh, Mani, Pramod, Dubey, Baokar, Gaurav & the whole lot of Cera-11 batch. Whether it was bunking classes or passing monstrous exams, they were always supportive.

I am also thankful to friends from Kota—Anjumon, Nirala, Anupam, Amit, Abhishek, Mouli, Murari, Vibash, Chaitanya, Rahul, Harshita, Anjali & Shikha.

The whole batch of Cands-05, RKMV, Deoghar deserves my thanks. Naimat, Chandan, Prateek, Shubham, Amrit, Ravi, Karn, Niraj, Manish, Pushpam, Anindya, Pritesh & Raman and others were great support.

I am grateful to Vineeth bhaiya for his invaluable input to the book.

I would like to thank the publishing and editorial team of Mahaveer Publishers, especially Azeem Ahmad Khan and Dilip Jha, for their unconditional support.

Above all, I am grateful to my parents, Kumud bhaiya, Rima didi, Rina didi and two wonderful brothers-in-law for their support and faith in me.

At times when the road looked like a dead-end, the Almighty came to the rescue.

There are so many people behind my dream. It helps me dream more and more.

A Word or Two

Love is a song, sing it.
Open your arms and embrace it.
Wherever you go, whatever you do
Never close your eyes for love can fly.
It is pure, it's gentle, and it's eternal.
It is everywhere and it can be nowhere.

Love is beautiful. And so is life. The beauty of life lies in appreciating good things and ignoring the bad. Learn to celebrate every single moment spent with loved ones. Happiness lies inside you, not outside.

Happy reading!

Priyesh Ranjan
(2priyeshranjan@gmail.com)

Chapter One

Letter, Parting & Going to Kota

Everything was like a dream. Three months ago, I was at the nadir of despair. I wanted to run away from everything. All my chances of making a great career had been ripped apart. No one, but I, was to blame. My story—a paradigm of absolute failure—got a paradigm shift, all thanks to the Midas touch of divine forces. I must say, life is like a dance where the beats decide your steps.

I looked at the watch. It was 5:30 p.m. No one in his right mind would like to be stuck in a room especially when he or she is staying in a seaside resort, a few steps away from a enticing beach.

Four days in Goa and I had already fallen for the place. I had already made a decision to buy a villa there as soon as I amassed enough fortune. Even Bharti thought the same. That is the only place in the country where Nature is in full glory, the landscape is luscious and people party round the clock.

For the last one hour, I had been trying to put things in the right order. I had the usual habit of making things messy. Only this time I wanted to pull it off. One more day and Bharti and I could create history.

I called up Bharti.

"When is our flight?"

"10'o clock. We leave for the airport at eight."

"Okay. See you then," I said and hung up.

I took a coffee mug and went out in the porch. The palpable pain in my legs made sitting a better option. My phone beeped.

'*Man, U & Bharti make a gr8 pair. U guys deserve nothing less than the best. All d luck.*'

It was an SMS from Vivek. Ever since I got close to winning, my inbox has been flooded with messages from relatives, friends and a few unknown people. Fame is like a flower; the fragrance attracts. But an important name was missing from my inbox—Aditi. The grave misunderstanding between us had turned things pretty sour. Last time we had talked was a month ago. The fault was not mine; her overreaction was to blame.

I took out a pinkish paper from my wallet. Watermarks of roses ran all across it. The charm of Aditi's petite handwriting mellowed some stress in my head.

Dear Abhi

You are the best possible gift I ever got. You entered my life like a breeze. Sweetly and smoothly! I fell in love with you. Wow! What a wonderful experience it has been since then! And now, I love you more than my life. I have watched love stories in movies, read about love in books and heard a lot from others, but it was you who made me feel what it is really about. No other emotion can ever be purer, gentler or sweeter. For some, love is just a word; for some it's their only world.

I looked at the sky. The stillness of dusk was still there. The sun was kissing goodbye to the ocean, promising to kiss it again at dawn. The breeze was reveling. I continued reading.

Today, when I look back at our journey, I realise there are some things, like our first date, first kiss, first dance and many more which are immortal. I am grateful to you for making such things possible.

I truly believe that a person grows the most when he or she is in love. I don't need the moon or the stars. For me they no longer matter as long as I have you. I am incomplete without you.

Everyone is, without their love. When you hold my hands, I feel like a princess. I love those naughty stares of yours. Talking over phone for hours, those beautiful SMSes, eating out with you, watching a movie together, romancing in a park—all these fill colour in my life and to add to those, are our silly stupid fights, tears in eyes and then missing each other terribly. When you are not around, I miss you a lot. A lot!

All of us look for love, but only a few are fortunate to find it. And fewer are able to retain it. Most importantly, only the fewest get them back in the next many births. Dear, I pray to God to put me in the last category. On this Valentine's Day, I promise to be with you always and ever. Till my last breath; I love you!

Yours Aditi.

Aditi had given me this letter on the last Valentine's Day. After reading it, I felt a void in my heart. The feeling made me restless. To bounce back, I travelled in the past. The lanes of memories were nostalgic, sweet, bitter and salty! A *masala* mix!

Sixteen Months Back; May; Last Year

"475," a female voice on the other side screamed.

"Wowoooooo! 95 per cent! Amazing! Congrats. It was well done."

"Yeah, I am feeling right at the top of the world!" Shruti exclaimed.

"Sure, you worked hard, so you deserved it. So, when's the party? Let us meet in the afternoon. This time I want a big treat."

"Hey! Why not now?" she suggested.

"Okay! See you in twenty minutes at the Garden restaurant," I said and hung up. "Mummy, Shruti got 95 per cent."

"I always knew. What a gem she is. So, she must be the topper of the school?" my mother asked.

"Yeah, as expected."

"What about your other friends?"

"Everyone managed to score well with a few exceptions."

My mother gave me a look as if I belonged to the latter category. I hated those you-did-not-perform look of hers. I scored 85 per cent, but that was too far from good for her. She was unhappy, may be because my score would let her down in the next kitty party. Unlike her, I was pretty happy and satisfied with my marks. I loved my mother a lot but when it came to academics, I could never please her. She always expected a good performance from me; after all, I was the youngest son of an IIT-plus-IIM-graduate father.

"Abhi, did you tell your father about the result?"

"Yes, I did and he was happy unlike you," I expressed my dissatisfaction.

"Oh really, he is the one who gave you so much of freedom."

"Please Mom, don't start it again," she glanced at me as her eyes bulged out in anger. "I am going out to meet Shruti and will be back by the evening," I glanced at her from the corner of my right eye. Before she could start the cruel song of my relative underperformance, I walked out of the house. Believe me; I would prefer to attend a spiritual discourse rather than listen to that cruel song. Why do people take academics so seriously? For some it's like a matter of life and death. Bullshit! Wise words are sometimes bitter; or always, if they are directed at you!

Shruti, my best friend, was an exception to the famous saying that a girl can only be either beautiful or intelligent. We have known each other for the last ten years. In fact, I was witness to the making of the beauty who had recently turned 18. 16 is sweet, 17 is sweeter and 18 is the sweetest. Girls in the class envied Shruti's beauty.

There were seven things which made our journey of friendship special. Shruti aptly termed it the recipe for great *fun-dosting.*

- We met for the first time when we were in third standard. On that very day I ate her tiffin, leaving her hungry and in tears. Our class teacher punished me with detention and my mother had to apologise to Shruti's parents. All due to *aloo paranthas*!
- In the initial years we fought over small issues. Yes, I

still remember the day when we were in the fourth standard. I had slapped her five times to settle the score of a pinch she had gifted me. Our parents were tired of our stupid acts but they could hardly do anything.

- During the fifth standard, we played the roles of a prince and princess at our annual function. After the play, I kissed her on the cheek. Yes, in fifth standard! Of course, the inspiration was '*Kuch Kuch Hota Hain*'. Things changed for us since then.
- Three years later we were the first in the class who started bunking school to go and see movies. At the same time, we became experts at using swear words. While all this continued, Shruti kept on excelling at studies while my academic graph went down.
- During the tenth standard, there was a teacher whom we despised a lot. On Teacher's Day we sent him a punch-box concealing the sender's identity. We used the identity of another boy with whom I was not on good terms. The plan worked. The teacher's nose got fractured and the boy ended up being suspended. We termed it as the Oscar-winning moment of our life.
- We matured as friends in eleventh class. One night, I happened to stay at her house. We talked for hours. The topics of discussion were periods, sex and autoeroticism.

We transgressed all degrees of frankness. And before your perverted mind cooks up anything, let me tell you that we slept on two different beds and didn't intend to do anything that what we talked of. Many gossips were cooked regarding our romantic involvement. But I and Shruti shared a platonic relationship. There was not an ounce of romance. That's all! Only after that night we could talk anything including, non-veg jokes. Our inboxes were full of them.

- All these years, Shruti saved my ass umpteen number of times times. We also exchanged numerous friendship cards, 'Sorry' and 'Miss You cards'. I certainly had the larger collection. The most unique thing about us was that on every Friendship Day, we observed a fast but ate only chocolates to neutralise the acids that filled our stomachs.

If you think that our recipe of *fun-dosting* had all the Bollywood *masala*, then wait a second. You didn't think anything different. Even Shruti and I thought the same.

There is a peculiar thing about friends. You can fight with them, hate them, miss them, envy them, but you can't live without them. You need them just to survive. Shruti was the most special amongst all my friends.

When I reached Garden restaurant, Shruti was already waiting.

"Hi, Shru, looking gorgeous!"

"You are late."

"I am a guest to your party and isn't the host supposed to wait for the guest?"

"Okay Mr Witty, let's have some food. I am starving."

"Your facial expression insinuates that the ghost of periods is haunting you. C'mon Ma'am, smile. You have scored fantastic," I remarked.

"Shut up!" she tweaked my ears.

"I can understand the pain," I continued with the wisecracking.

"You stupid! Dare you say anything and I'll crush your balls," she threatened.

"Okay, I give up. I won't allow you to do the honour," I winked and smiled.

We walked inside the Garden restaurant. It was one of the classy and quietest places in the city whose high gastronomic quotient made it an ideal place for foodies like us.

"Abhi, day after tomorrow I would be leaving for Delhi," she said, as we occupied a corner table. Shruti had plans to move to Delhi for under-graduate studies. And now with the kind of marks she had achieved, all doors were open for her.

"That's great. What about the arrangements there?"

"My father's friend lives there. He will take care of it."

"Okay, go and start your innings and take care of

yourself. And most importantly, don't dare stay out of touch with me."

"Are you crazy? I am going to miss you a lot. You are my best friend and these ten years have made us inseparable. And how can I forget our recipe of great *fun-dosting?*"

For the next half an hour we went into retrospective mood, recollecting sweet memoirs from our past. We talked about our friendship, about numerous stupid fights we had, about sacrifices we made for each other and the way ahead.

Around 8 p.m., I returned home. Everybody was in the living room and were discussing me. Obviously it was related to my result and my future plans.

"So what have you thought next?" Papa looked straight into my eyes. I always wanted to be like him—an IIT plus IIM graduate.

"Papa, I want to be an IITian like you. This year I was ill-prepared for IIT exams. I still have a chance and I want to devote this year for preparations." My last sentence struck silence in the room.

My Dad, a successful entrepreneur, moved to the city of steel, Jamshedpur, 25 years ago. He was a busy man but always managed to spend quality time with his children. Unlike Mummy, he was liberal in most of the matters and always encouraged me to follow my heart. No doubt, he was more of a friend than a parent.

"Okay," Dad said. I had been confident that he would endorse my decision but still a tinge of fear is always associated when it comes to career decisions.

"So which institute would you like to join for coaching?" Mother asked.

"Some people have advised me to go to Kota. They say that coaching classes there have a high success rate. I am considering that option."

I knew my mother would not like the idea. No mother wants her child to stay away from her. But after an hour long debate, I was allowed to go ahead with the 'Kota' idea. As expected, my mother was still against it.

The next few days passed in making enquiries about the city, the institute in which I would be taking admission etc. I left no stones unturned in extracting the best information that I could. Relatives, friends, seniors, magazines, sites of institutes, Orkut and facebook—I did a thorough research. An excitement stepped up within me with every bit of detail I gathered about the city.

* * *

I still remember Mummy's tears on my shoulders while she hugged me at the railway junction. "Mummy, I am going just for a few days. Don't cry like that. I'll get back soon. Do take care of your health," I consoled her as the train whistled aloud.

"Keep a look out on your luggage and eat properly," she

said, kissing my forehead. I felt bestowed with tons of affection.

For the first time in my life I was going away from my family. My mind was occupied with thousands of thoughts. I realised the importance of family bonding. I thought about my friends, my relatives, my teachers, my neighbours. I thought of Kota, the people there, the environment and how I would adjust to the new place. In my entire train journey, thoughts kept crossing my mind just as the wind kept crossing the window panes. The train ran like greased lightning and so did my thoughts.

After a weary 30-hour journey, I reached the city which is referred to as the Mecca of education. For people like us, we called it as Kota. It was located on the prime Delhi-Mumbai rail route. On the very first day, my perceptions about Kota got a complete make-over. You would fall in love with this city at first glance, not because of any scenic beauty for it docs not have much, but there is a charisma around it. Those who have lived there know it better.

New place, new people, new environment, new lifestyle—with so many new things in my mind I took the first step of my new journey. I was nervous and had many qualms.

The initial two days at Kota passed like wind. Finding food, lodging and settling down in a new room with unknown faces all around was not easy. I was still an adolescent.

Life becomes tough at times. Rather, very tough. At least that was how things shaped up for me at that point of time.

"Take the change," the shopkeeper said as he handed over some coins to me.

That was my third day in the city. And I had been formally introduced to almost all the thorns that lay on my way. Yes, thorns—scorching heat coupled with an inefficient/poor cooler, insipid food, bitter taste of water. They were the major.

With three poly-bags in my hand and heebie-jeebies in my belly, I walked towards Gyan Vihar. That was where I was supposed to spend my next one year for preparation of IIT entrance exam. The better part was that there were hundreds like me. Sooner or later I was going to know a lot of them.

"Abhi, is everything all right?" Mr Jaiswal asked.

"Yes Uncle. Everything is fine."

Mr Jaiswal, my landlord, was a tall man. His strongly-built physique and dense moustache complemented his persona. He was empathetic and a nice man. He and his family lived on the ground floor while my room was on the first floor. A medium-sized room with a small balcony. The interior was of average look but the exterior facade of the house was genuinely glamorous. There were six other rooms on the first floor, all identical. Though the rent was high, still it was worth the facilities that were provided.

It was 7:30 p.m. I was very tired, so I sprawled on the bed. Next day was the orientation and welcome lecture at Apex Classes. The institute claimed to have the highest number of selections in IIT-JEE. Anyway, that was the last thing on my mind at that time. I was nearly done with the arrangement of the room. My mind was full of thoughts. Many things kept coming to my mind, especially the way my life had responded in last few days.

A sudden knock at the door got me out of my thoughts. It was 8 p.m. The mess boy stood with the tiffin at the door. In Kota, messes are as abundant as betel shops in any Indian city. I had encountered at least 15 during the last 72 hours. After a prima facie search, I joined 'Quality Mess'. I think the name forced me to do so, though the food was a great distortion from that image.

I swallowed *puri-sabzi* which was simply horrible. I cursed whosoever made that crap. My mother was zillion times a better cook.

After having dinner, I stretched out on the bed and kept thinking about the new life that was waiting for me till my eyes closed for the dreamy world.

Joker's Jottings

Have a lot of girls in your life. Believe me, it feels macho to have options. Girls don't need the advice. They are the wiser sex and have been playing multi-boying games for eons.

Discover your 'Shruti' aka best friend and find occasions to hug and kiss her. And if you get a chance, then move to a place like Kota to celebrate the liberty of ripened adolescence.

Chapter Two

Dosti, INSP & Stupid Test

"Well, you all know that IIT-JEE is one of the toughest entrance exams, and to crack it, you need a lot of things in the right place. You have chosen the right institute for your preparations, but remember the path ahead is thorny. You need a dogged pursuit and the highest level of sincerity to succeed. Beware of the slips. Even one wrong step can take you fathoms below the surface...."

A well-rehearsed and an effective speech! That was what the head of Apex Institute was delivering in front of all new students. His peculiar parlance and elegance created an absolute motivational ambience. I saw the whole class grasping each and every syllable with pin-drop silence. With so many new faces, I knew many friendships were on the cards. All this while, my eyeballs kept searching for some pretty faces. But all girls were engrossed in books, leaving my eyes hungry.

After attending the welcome lecture, I returned to my room with a lot of new books and some study sheets doled out by the institute. The arrival of study material dressed my room completely. Ostensibly, books are the biggest accessory of a student. I was pretty rejuvenated and ready to jump into the fight—the fight for the best, not just within the students of a city, but the entire country! That is what an IITian stands for. For a layman, an IITian is that lucky member of *Homo sapiens* who has a high IQ and a higher cash affinity, thereby ensuring a very bright survival with an entire gamut of pleasures. Go and ask any common man and this would be the most common answer.

I skimmed through the first few pages of a handbook. The bold letters on the opening page grabbed my attention.

Dream of getting high rank in IIT-JEE, and your life will get a new meaning. But remember that there are thousands like you. Last year more than 2.5 lakh students appeared in IIT-JEE. Six thousand were selected, out of which 1,000 were from Apex. The words of the head of my institute echoed in my ears. I felt proud to be a part of this institute. And somewhere down the head, it gave me a feeling of comfort and assurance that I was with the best. After all, your company decides your fate.

So what followed for the next one month was a very tight study schedule. There were loads of home assignments which left no time for respite. During the first few weeks, I did feel homesick on a couple of occasions. I missed my family, my mother's culinary skills and a lot of small things which were no longer small. Meanwhile, Shruti got admission in the Shri Ram College of Commerce. She was very happy about it and was enjoying her college days to the fullest. We used to exchange a lot of SMSes. Most of them carried the cliché—'I miss U' slogan. I really missed her. A lot!

Adaption is one of the basic instincts of the human kind. If voids are created, then they get filled too. I got familiar with my batch-mates. But in particular, I struck a chord with Vivek, Rohan and Naidu. We four formed a gang. Each one of us was different but we shared a certain equation which brought us together. As it happens in every gang, there was a cynosure, the soul. In our case it was me, Mr Rock Star of the gang.

Vivek was from Noida. His father, like mine, was an IIT graduate and worked as a senior manager in an MNC. His strapping body always made him noticeable and perhaps that was the best feature he had. Hunk or stud—that was what he usually boasted himself of. Vivek and Naidu shared a room in the boys' hostel.

J.S. Naidu was basically from Andhra Pradesh but he lived in Chandigarh. His father was a colleague of Vivek's father. With stooping shoulders, oily skin and skinny body, Naidu had contrasting features to his room-mate. Kilos of *jugaad* and ounces of crackpot—that was what Naidu was made of. Rohan, like me, lived as a paying guest. He was from Bhillai, another city famous for steel plants and located in Chhattisgarh. A very gracious and sophisticated person, Rohan's chubbiness made him look adorable. He was Mr Wise Ass of our gang.

We four were in the same batch, which was fourth from the top. Batches, as is the tradition of Kota, were classified on the basis of merit. Each batch consisted of 60 to 70 students on an average. I was happy that 11 more batches trailed mine. After all, competition is always relative!

"Guys, next Sunday, we have a test," Naidu said in an apprehensive tonc. His accent was peculiar and it announced his southern connection.

"Bro, I have never studied this much. Still I am unable to complete my assignments," Vivek said with a what-are-you-saying-mother-fucker look. Frustration was evident on his face.

"By the way, what is the syllabus and mode of the test?" I asked.

"It would be objective-cum-subjective and the course taught till last week is the syllabus," Naidu replied.

"Comrades, let me tell you the main thing. This is going to be a fucking shuffling test. Our batches will be shuffled on the basis of our performances," Rohan made an important disclosure.

"Don't you think that these guys are *chutiyas*? They don't teach the concepts with clarity, keep on giving enormous home-work and now they are so keen on taking the shit out of us."

We gave mute support to Vivek's statement and simultaneously increased the speed of our bicycles. Batch shuffling was very important for all of us. The better we perform, greater the chances of being in the top batch. Who doesn't want to be in the top league? But hundreds of other students must be thinking the same. The thought further heightened the speed of my cycle. Jealousy and competition are sisters. Hardly a month had passed and the unwanted ghost had arrived as a test.

At night, I had a chat with Shruti for an hour. She kept talking for most of the time. No man can beat a girl when it comes to gossip. She told me about her college, her new friends and an assortment of things that had taken place in the last few days. Now that we were distant, we felt each other's importance.

The next five days passed like wind. I was totally absorbed in the preparations. Two days before the test, we four held a

discussion session. It lasted for hours. We talked about various mind-boggling concepts and cross-questioned each other. I could easily say that Rohan was the sharpest among us and Naidu was his opposite. Anyhow, we honed our preparations. Before we parted, we planned a trip to movie after the test. We had been working hard for the last five weeks and it was high time we went for a break.

The night before the test, I got nearly half a dozen SMSes wishing me luck. All of them were from Shruti. Reading those definitely eased my nervousness a little bit.

How would a tenth standard student react to a twelfth standard question paper? That was exactly what I was feeling during the test. I was not alone. My neighbours were also in the same shocked state. I could not even attempt half of the questions. As I came out of the room, Rohan, Vivek and Naidu were already waiting for me. No surprise—their faces were gloomy. Everyone was silent till we reached the cycle-stand.

"The paper was a complete *gaand-phaadu*. I think I will score hardly 30% marks," I broke the silence. Nobody said anything but gave me a *meri-tujhse-jyada-phati* look. I thought it was useless to inquire about their performances. The dejected expression on their faces said everything.

"*Saale*, if we perform like this, then very soon we are going to be demoted to the last batch. The content of the

course and the level of questions get tougher with time," Naidu let out his frustration.

Three years back, Naidu's elder brother qualified in IIT-JEE. He had done coaching at Apex. So whatever Naidu said ought to be authentic. And his latest caveat was building anxiety in us. But nothing was in our hands.

We reached Kota Cineplex at 3 p.m. Tickets for the matinee show had already been booked. None of us was in a mood to celebrate. But on account of the monotonous life and preoccupation with studies, a break was the need of the hour. Besides, a movie could help us forget what had happened in the morning. All of us were in doldrums and hoped that the movie could work as our saviour. All this while we had left no stones unturned in cursing the teacher, who had set the question paper. For us, he was a tormentor, a devil.

"Boys, complaining will only exacerbate the situation. Let us forget all this rubbish and have some fun," Rohan tried to bring the celebratory vibe. We seconded his suggestion.

Kota Cineplex, or KCP as popularly known, was a nice multiplex located in the heart of the city. The day being a holiday, the whole place teemed with people. We bought popcorns and took our seats. The Hollywood flick was a complete entertainer. Its special effects were mesmerising. But the only spoilsport was the immature dubbing, which was really funny at places. We enjoyed our time thoroughly. During the film my eyeballs found a source of diversion. The source was a girl sitting in the front row. Her babyish style of talking caught my attention. Her cute laughter further reinforced my stare. After the show, I could not resist myself from trailing her. But unfortunately, she vanished like a flame. I kept roaming with eyes wide open. Finally my eyes grabbed her near a restaurant. She was with her friends. Wearing a black satin suit, she looked gorgeous. Her slim figure, fair skin, pierced ears, petite nose, luscious lips and stimulating assets—everything made her an eye-candy. Who says that angels wear only white? The angel in front of me was in black. Beauty was not in her but in the beholder's eye. When she walked inside the restaurant, I took notice of her stilettos. The girl was classy and chic. A complete package!

Naidu finally found me near the restaurant.

"Okay, now where do we go for dinner?" Rohan asked. Every Sunday night, messes in Kota remained closed; so we were supposed to eat out.

"Let us go to Strawberry," I suggested.

Everybody nodded. That was the place where Miss Beauty had gone. I thought going there would give me an opportunity for NSP. NSP (*Nainsukh prapti*) was our code language for staring at chicks. There were many more codes that we used; in fact nowadays the whole world uses them.

We took a table adjacent to the one where Miss Beauty was sitting with her friends. I kept giving intermittent glances to their table. By now my friends were aware of my real intention of coming to the restaurant.

"*Kameenay*, now I understood why you brought us here so that you can stare at that *maal*," Naidu nudged me.

We thoroughly enjoyed our time even though the food was not that good. I was cursed for that. Then we started the real talk—it was girls. Finally we were in a mood. I must say that more than 80 per cent of the time boys either talk about girls (*read romance and physical aspects*) or gadgets. I don't know about girls, but boys' interest lies in double-sided G-word: girls and gadgets. The sad part of my NSP was that the girl didn't notice me even once. Even though bespectacled, I had looks any girl would find appealing. Shruti always told me that other girls in our class were jealous of her as she spent a lot of time with me. I assumed the compliment to be equivalent to the Nobel Prize.

By the time I returned, the main gate of the house was closed. After an anxious 10-minute wait, which was followed by some bossy queries by Jaiswal Uncle, I was allowed to enter the house. As soon as I entered my room, my phone rang. Shruti was on the other side. I told her about my test. She opened the consolation box and said a lot of nice things to make me feel like a champ. I loved to share things with her.

When I told her about the NSP girl, I felt a tinge of jealousy in her tone. The joyful chat lasted 15 minutes. Unlike my mother, Shruti always supported me on the academic ground. She even tutored me before the XII standard Board exam. I owed a lion's share of my percentage to her. My mother always had high expectations from me. Alas! I couldn't do anything great in academics.

I reclined on the chair and allowed thoughts to invade me. It was not the result, but that girl on my mind. I was obsessed with her.

On the next day, in the class, we were told the solutions of the test paper. If questions were hard to comprehend, solutions were even harder to absorb. A few students in the top batch had scored more than 80% marks and some of them had even achieved cent per cent in chemistry. Though a few questions were easy, still it was incredible even to think of 80% in chemistry.

We were told that the results would be announced on the coming Monday. The next one week passed in anxiety. In between my mother queried a lot about my score and the performance of others. She always kept harping on the same do's and don'ts saga. The wait was really getting longer. Finally the 'result day' arrived. I rushed to the institute's administrative building in the morning. The whole region near the notice-board was swarming with students. There

were lots of noises, exclamations and confusions. It was really hard to figure out one's score. My eyes finally got it.

Abhi Sharma....physics-17....chemistry-25....maths-20....Total-62....Rank-700.

O my God! I am screwed. What am I going to do with this score? Mummy is going to kill me. I was dejected, disheartened and worried on seeing the result. But this was bound to happen. I came out of the institute building as quickly as possible. A strong dislike for everything around me filled my heart. Absolute frustration!

In the evening, I went to Vivek's place. Like me, he was also unhappy with his result. Vivek and Naidu had secured ranks near 900. Though Rohan got a rank of 300, I must say that he deserved much better. We whimpered for hours and drew some sort of joy in complaining about irrelevant things. We celebrated our underperformance by grumbling and awarding our teachers with swearwords. Strange, but the exercise proved to be a breather and at that time the breather became the source of survival.

Two days later our batches were shuffled. No wonder I was demoted to the eighth batch. While Rohan succeeded in retaining his, Vivek and Naidu moved down to twelfth batch. The result had two implications. First, my mother became stricter than ever. She didn't want her son to be a loser. Second, I became more conscious of my studies. I cut the leisure time and studied harder. But the real fallout was somewhere else. Deep down in the head, I started losing self-esteem and depression stayed there. I had never faced so brutal a brunt of competition. I knew I was no topper material but I wanted to be an achiever. The thoughts of Miss Beauty stayed dormant in some corner of my mind.

Joker's Jottings

Amass enough fortunes to buy a girls' college or hostel-facing flat. Then shift your bedroom to the balcony. Guys, remember lack of NSP can lead to defective eyes. Please, help your eyes. Maal hi to *nature* ka kamaal hai!

And a noteworthy advice to girls: don't apply so much make-up on your face. You better know where boys' glances visit first. Don't you?

Chapter Three

Her Taciturnity & Pyjama Party

Time passes very quickly if you are involved in something. The next test was two weeks away. I was fully determined to perform this time. After the first batch shuffling I was demoted. I wanted to see myself in the top batch. All four of us now attended classes in different batches, thereby disabling us from spending more time together. Still, whenever we met, we discussed about the teachers of our batches, their pedagogy, girls in our classes and our inefficiency in solving sums which were monstrous for us. These sums, as it appeared, were not designed for us but the teacher who took pride in solving them.

My friendship with Vivek, Naidu and Rohan grew with time. We began to know more about each other. Almost every evening we met at Raju's tea-stall which was an official *adda* of our group. Raju Bhaiya was a nice man and his tea even tasted better.

"You know, I miss my girlfriend," One day Rohan shared his feeling with us at our *adda*.

"Are you committed?" I was surprised with the revelation. Rohan was a very serious student; kind of matured and academically focused. I never knew about the romantic side to his personality.

"I am, since XI standard. I love Neha, my sweetheart," he replied.

"*Phodu*! What does she do?" Naidu asked.

"She just took admission in a commerce college," he gave us an I-love-her-a-lot look and blushed. He showed us her photo. Written on the back of the photo was: '*My sweetheart, my darling, my sexy angel, muah muah.*'

Rohan was only 17 plus and had a girlfriend. If one of your friends has a girl and you don't, then you feel like a loser. Human psychology! The closest girl I had in my life was Shruti.

Were I and Shruti just friends? I missed having my own girl. Have patience, I thought.

Next Saturday, a very interesting thing happened with me.

Naidu and I went to a cyber café for a movie. Naidu was completely net savvy. He had an addiction and didn't mind spending the whole day sitting in front of a computer. I believe, for most of us, internet is all about some social networking sites, online flirting, porn and movies. I hate those guys who say that internet is a source of obscenity and immoral values. Does it matter any longer? Be happy and nothing matters; be unhappy and everything is a source of trouble. Besides, if there is a demand, then there has to be supply. This is the basics of economics.

"*Saale*, see her. Your *maal*! There she is sitting," Naidu whispered with a nudge.

Ah! There sat my movie girl. Wearing an orange top, she was looking awesome. Her elegance made it hard to ignore her. The beatific face was as cheery as the day. I could not take my eyes off the cabin she was sitting in. Forgetting all my manners, I tried to peep at her screen. She was browsing facebook. I took a cabin diagonal to her. The cyber cafes in Kota inquire into identity as a pre-emption to any cyber irregularities—one of the fucking rules. I knew Naidu was a regular at that café and was well acquainted with the café-owner.

"Naidu, do me a favour. Find out her identity from the log register," I said with was desperation on my face.

Five minutes later he returned with a victorious smile.

All this while, I kept staring at my Miss Beauty. The pleasure of watching girls is heavenly; you just don't get bored.

"Your in-laws live in Dehradun and your sweetheart's name is Aditi Agarwal," he shared the victory with me.

This was all I needed. Within a few minutes I found out her profile on facebook and explored every corner of it. She was in XII standard, one year junior to me and studied at Toppers Institute. Toppers Institute was one of the many institutes of Kota. The devil inside me began to work. Acting on an impulse, I sent her a friendly request. But to my amusement, I got a refusal within five minutes. A straight 'no!'

"What to do now?" I asked Naidu.

"In my view, go and talk to her directly."

"But how do I start?"

"Do it anyhow. At least she will notice you."

I finally resolved to make a direct approach to her. When Aditi left the café, she was alone. I thought it to be the most opportune time. I signalled Naidu to stay at the café. I walked briskly and accosted her near a sweet shop.

"Hi! I am Abhi Sharma; from Jamshedpur," I said.

I looked direct into her eyes. The *kajal* in her eyes made it worth observing. She gave me an offended look as if I had trespassed upon her privacy.

"I am from Apex. I was the one who sent you a request," I continued boldly.

"So, didn't I turn it down?" she retorted. The girl was smart.

"Excuse me."

Before I could say anything, she started walking. I glanced at her features which were too sharp to ignore. Mouthwatering, I would say. Suddenly the phone rang.

"Hello Bro, what happened?" Naidu was on the other side.

"Nothing good. She walked away."

It was not the kind of meeting I expected it to be. I had already fallen for the girl and the big question disturbing me was, what's next? I returned to my room with lots of thoughts.

At 11 p.m., Shruti's call woke me up from Aditi's thoughts.

"Hi Shru, what's up?"

"Abhi, you won't believe what happened today," she almost screamed. Before I could say anything, she continued in her elated tone, "A guy proposed to me. He is an amazing guy. And you know, I said 'yes' to him. I am very happy today. I have sent you his snaps. Check your mail-box."

"It's great news. So finally someone stole my angel," I didn't know why I said so. Maybe I was not happy. Was I possessive of Shruti? Maybe! After all, she was my best friend.

"No man, nobody comes in between our friendship."

"Yeah, I know. So, who is that lucky guy?"

"Prateek Khanna. He is a nice guy. I think we both make a great couple."

That night we kept talking for more than an hour. Prateek, Shruti's boyfriend, was her immediate senior in college. For the whole time she kept telling things about him. I had no other option but to listen.

History repeats itself, even under different circumstances. The second test was worse than the first one. The questions were even more *phaadu*! I had put in a lot of effort but all turned fruitless. Why? An unsolved mystery!

The same night, I went to Vivek's place. We had planned a pyjama party. Every celebration has a cause. In our case we tried hard to figure out a cause but we didn't succeed. Perhaps escapism from the mundane things of our lives, especially dismal performance, could be a reason. We belonged to the same basket of bastards. Our friendship matured faster with every passing day. I think that usually happens when you are at the threshold of adulthood, bidding goodbye to adolescence.

"Vivek, I think this time I am coming to your batch," I said in a sad tone.

"Oye *Rondu*, don't worry, this time there will be no batch shuffling. It is scheduled every alternate test," Vivek patted my shoulders and made me feel like I missed an Olympic gold by a very small margin.

"Leave all those rubbish things. See what I have brought for you," said the mischievous Naidu with beer cans in his hands. The smile on his face was that of a Nobel Prize winner.

I had never tasted beer until I was in XII standard. The fervour and excitement of drinking at an age when you are supposed to be sincere to studies attracts most youngsters towards it. Girls and drinking have two things in common—addiction and pleasure. There is no harm in it if you are careful and stay within limits.

Like me, Vivek and Naidu were also experienced players. Rohan was a novice and we had to prod him a lot to join the drinkers' league.

"Guys, you know, our teachers at Apex are not humans, but butchers," Naidu gave a vent to his feelings.

"*Ghatiya*, *bakwaas* and *madhar*. They enjoy putting bamboos in our asses. Can't they teach and set questions properly," I joined Naidu's side.

"Don't spoil the mood by talking about them," Vivek suggested.

"True Bro, when I was in school, I had a few teachers who were ridiculous;" Naidu said and continued, "there was a teacher who had the habit of speaking absolutely funny English. At one occasion he asked me 'to shut door, when he wanted the window shut' and on the other, he fumingly threatened by saying, 'I'll catch you by the throat and jump out of the window'. The poor guy! We nick-named him English *chodu*."

We burst into laughter.

"This is nothing. I had one teacher in my school whose farts were sharper than our school bell. We used to tease him as *ghatak hamla*," Vivek bragged about his teacher's greatness. We carried on talking about our teachers' nerdish traits for a few more minutes until the dormant Miss Beauty inside me was awakened by my buddy.

"Abhi, what happened to your Aditi?" Vivek asked with a satirical smile. I liked the 'your' part. At least there was someone who acknowledged my feelings for Aditi.

"Nothing, I could not know anything more about her. Even I didn't manage to see her after that day."

"If she is from Toppers then she must be living in Bada Nagar. Why don't you look for her there?" Naidu suggested.

"Are you crazy? There are hundreds of girls there. It is as hard as shooting in the dark," I said.

I was eager to meet her again. Every single feature of her was still afresh in my memory. Her eyes, the *kajal*, her loveable nose, her circular danglers, her melodious voice, her tangible assets, everything!

All this while, Rohan was busy talking to Neha. After a few minutes, he was back with a smile on his face.

"What happened, Mr Drunken Lover? How is your darling?" I asked wistfully.

"Nothing. She is fine."

"So Mr Lover, can I ask you a question?" Vivek asked.

"Go ahead."

"Did you guys ever get physical?"

I did not understand why Vivek asked that question. I mean, it was too bold and too personal. I feared Rohan might have gotten offended by the query but to my surprise he stayed calm and unruffled.

"Yes, we did a few times."

We all smiled and looked at him. There was reverence and awe in our looks. Rohan was a real champ. Great achievement! Our generation is too fast and too demanding! He had done that which makes most of the guys roll out their tongues, and that too so early!

That night we slept at 5 a.m. We talked about our school lives, our families, our cities and indeed about G-world. Vivek showed us more than a dozen pictures of his girlfriend taken from his mobile, all showing her ass cracks explicitly. It took him two years of hard work to collect that. I wonder what linguist would term such a mania; ass-o-crack-philia maybe. With every moment we spent together, our bonding grew stronger. I was proud to have friends like them. But somewhere inside my mind, I was cooking a plan. I thought of giving a visit to Bada Nagar. Maybe I would succeed, I thought. There was hope...

Joker's Jottings

If one of your friends hangs out with his sexy chick, how do you feel? I know, smoke comes out of your ass and your heart bleeds. Stop being a Dhakkan. *Be brave, show the money and get a honey. Make sure you have some glory to brag; something like cinema hall smooches and groping, touch-game in parks. And for now, pray for me and Aditi. May I attain my glory!*

Chapter Four

Kismet Connection

The next week I was the victim of a double whammy. The first, as expected, was the dismal test results and the second one was a disappointing visit to Bada Nagar. Vivek and I went there for a rampant search. Though we came across several pretty faces, but none of them was that of Aditi. The only good part was that we got some quality NSP. From our visit we reached to a conclusion that Toppers Institute scored over Apex in the girls' department. One benefit of studying at Kota was you always have the opportunity to see beatific faces coming from all across the country. Something we call 'greenery' of the whole country.

Depression was endemic in my life. Whenever we four met, we kept whining and finding faults with the system. To kill the boredom and bleakness, Naidu and I frequently visited cyber cafes and play-stations. These were the hotspots for those who were repelled by studies. Movies and games kept students engrossed there.

I still remember September 1st. It was a Friday. Something happened which proved to be a milestone in my life. It was a call from my mother. The time was 9:30 p.m.

"Hello, son! How are you?" she asked the familiar question.

"Hi, Mom! I am fine. How are you?"

"I am okay. What about your studies? Are you working hard? See, this is your last chance. Your whole career depends on it."

"I know it."

I hated her customary discourse on do's and don'ts.

"But your performance doesn't show that you are studying hard."

"Don't worry Mom, I am wise enough."

"Okay. Well, do you remember Sheetal Aunty?"

"Yeah, I do. What happened?"

Sheetal Aunty was my Mom's very close friend during college days. They were students of JNU. Her stories of college life always included Sheetal Aunty as an integral part.

"Sheetal's daughter is also studying in Kota. She wants

you to meet her. I have given Sheetal your address and contact number. Her daughter might contact you."

"Okay, I will take care of it."

"Goodnight."

"Goodnight," I said and hung up.

The entire Sunday morning went in solving sums. Out of a hundred problems that we were supposed to solve, I could do only 40. *Saale sawaal nahi, haiwaan the!* Teachers enjoy killing students' holidays by making them rub their asses sitting in the chair. Around 5 p.m. my phone rang.

"Hello! Is it Abhi Sharma?" a very sweet voice on the other side asked.

"Yes. May I know who this is?" I was eager to know her identity.

"I am Mrs Sheetal Agrawal's daughter. You must be knowing her."

"Oh! I got you. I was expecting your call. So how are you?"

"I am fine. Are you free? Mom has asked me to meet you."

"Yeah, the pleasure will be mine."

"Come to the city coffee shop in 15 minutes. I will be waiting there."

"Okay. See you soon."

I was so entangled in my sums that I even forgot to ask her name. Anyway, I had her number. The city coffee shop

was in Bada Nagar. I had gone there along with Vivek on my maiden visit to Bada Nagar. The place was a hot destination for lovebirds and to-be lovebirds.

It took me 20 minutes to reach the place. As I got off the rickshaw, I got an absolute shocker. Aditi was standing in front of the coffee shop. My heart started running like a horse. *Is she Sheetal Aunty's daughter?* I walked hesitatingly toward her.

"Hi! I am Abhi Sharma. Are you Sheetal Aunty's daughter?" I tried to smile.

"Yes. I am. Aditi Agarwal from Dehradun," she exchanged a handshake.

"I am really delighted to meet you," I remarked.

"Me too. So how are you?'

"I am fine. Look, I am really sorry for that day. I didn't mean to offend you."

"No, it is all right. I think I was too rude. But you know, I cannot talk to any stranger like that. Anyway, let us forget that. How is aunty?"

"She is okay. Let us go inside."

We occupied a corner table and ordered two frappes.

"So, where do you live?"

"Gyan Vihar."

Aditi was dressed in a white *salwar* suit and as always, looked charming. I still couldn't believe the angel I had been

dreaming of was sitting right in front of me.

"I saw you that day in Kota cineplex. You were with your friends."

For many guy's, talking to a girl is a problem. But I was not one of them. I knew what appealed to girls; however, on that day I was a bit uncomfortable with Aditi. Maybe because I was stunned by the kismet connection or was I caught unprepared.

"Oh, that Hollywood flick! You know, I am a complete movie buff. Alas! I have not been there since that movie."

The waiter brought the frappes.

"So, did you like the city?" she asked.

"Yes, I love this place. I think it is a haven for students."

"Yeah."

"Did someone tell you that you are very beautiful?" I tried to be smart.

"Oho! Thanks for the compliment. By the way you are also not that bad," she giggled.

"I guess you won't reject my 'friend request' this time around," I said with a tongue-in-cheek look.

"Don't worry, I will send you one," she scored over me.

After having frappes we went for a walk. Aditi was well acquainted with the city. She had been living there for more than a year. She told me a lot about her past. The way she talked I felt as if we were friends since a long time. The only thing she did not discuss about was whether she had a boyfriend or not. I didn't expect her to reveal the secret in the first meet but I was very eager to know about it. Before bidding goodbye, I said, "Aditi! I really enjoyed every moment with you. You are really a sweet girl. I wish I had known you earlier."

At first, she stared at me. Perhaps she doubted the flirtatious nature of my remark. Then she laughed and replied, "So did I."

I am a fan of Paulo Coelho. In one of his books he wrote, "When you want to achieve something, then the whole world conspires with you to achieve that." That day the saying became a reality for me.

Thank you god for making Sheetal Aunty and my mother close friends.

I had already fallen for Aditi and things really got exciting with this serendipity. Our mothers wanted us to meet, God wanted us to meet. Implicitly it was a green signal from all corners.

Next day the breaking news hit Naidu, Vivek and Rohan. They didn't believe it at first and later they were amused.

"*Kutte*, you hit a jackpot. What a luck!" Vivek remarked wistfully.

"Come on, now we want a treat from you," Naidu demanded.

I didn't mind spending one thousand bucks for them. After all, they were also a part of the conspiracy. Later, Vivek urged me to stay overnight at his place, but I simply refused on account of the monstrous homework.

At 10:30 p.m. a knock disturbed my nap. To my surprise it was Jaiswal Uncle, my landlord. He was a very busy man and even though we lived in the same house, we had hardly seen each other in the last couple of days.

"So Abhi, how is everything?"

"Everything is fine, uncle," I replied.

"Your mother called me up this morning. She said that you are not performing well in exams. Do you have some problem?"

So here was the real intention of his visit. My mother worried a lot for my studies. She knew that I was playful and less committed to my studies. Does anyone love to study?

"No, Uncle. Everything is okay. Actually the course is too tough. They keep changing the format of questions every now and then; getting some problems in adapting to their pedagogy. I am working hard to secure good marks; a little bit of bad luck," I was a good orator in school and had a lot of awards to my credit. There is a very simple rule—of oratory if you have confidence and attitude, you can leave a long-lasting impression on the listener. Good oratory gives an edge at convincing others with your masked truth.

"Last year one of my tenants secured a rank within five hundred. I hope that you too would excel like him," he looked convinced with my fibs. He moved towards the door.

"And one more thing, you guys make a lot of noise. Do celebrate, but take care that others are not disturbed," he said in an imperious tone.

I knew he was pointing at what happened three days ago. There were six more students living in Jaiswal Villa. Four of them were medical aspirants and two were AIEEE aspirants. That day we were celebrating the birthday of one of the medical guys. Birthday bumps, cake all over our faces, loud music and rowdy dance; we created a razzmatazz. We had played a Punjabi hit for more than 10 times.

Surat niraali, man ki tu kaali……jhooth mat bol ki kala kauwa kaat khayega….

There was a peculiar thing about this song. At every marriage party and at every celebration in Kota, the song was religiously played at least half a dozen times. I always wondered why the song had the reputation as 'the song' of the city! The overall result of our mischief was that the neighbours called up our landlord. And at 1:30 a.m. our landlady, who was also a victim of our celebration, became our predator. The celebration ended on a sad note with her half-an-hour long discourse. She threatened to inform our parents. We called her bluff and ignored it. Fortunately she did not.

Joker's Jottings

Still Single? Never forget to visit your mother's college friends. Maybe you will bump into their hot daughters! Socialise and keep hunting till you get a damsel to play with your balls. Remember, kismet favours the opportunist.

Chapter Five

Mechanics, Mantras and the Bengali Chick

"Hello Aditi! What's up? How are you doing?"

"I am fine. What about you?"

Just 48 hours had passed after the serendipitous meet, but it felt like we hadn't for months. She had climbed to the top of my priority list.

"I am okay and having fun. But you seem quite busy. No reply. No SMS," I said.

I had sent her more than 20 messages in the last two days. But to my disappointment, she didn't reply even once.

"Oh! I am really sorry. Actually the semester exam is round the corner, so quite engaged in my studies. Anyway,

those SMSes were really funny and naughty. I liked them," she chuckled.

"Thanks for the compliment. Hey, the latest Bollywood flick is releasing this Friday. I hope you don't mind if I ask you to it. My treat."

She had told me about her interest in movies and I had already planned a lot to score with that.

"Well, I cannot promise you. I will have to think," she replied.

"Okay! Wish you all the luck for your exams. I will wait for your reply," I said and hung up.

Half an hour later I again sent her an SMS. I wanted to leave no stones unturned to make my entry and presence marked in her life. Thankfully this time she replied. I read it a dozen times before Vivek's call spoilt the fun of it.

"Hello Abhi! We will be there in 15 minutes. Be ready."

"Okay."

We were going to a Punjabi *dhaba*. The *dhaba* was well known for its economical yet gourmet food. The exercise was a part of Naidu's birthday treat. Last night we gave him bumps, GPL and now he was treating us. What a strange celebration a birthday is!

The food was really delicious. One's stay at Kota is incomplete without a visit to the Punjabi *Dhaba*. The food simply rocks. There were a few more guys from Naidu's hostel. I was familiar with all of them. In a city like Kota, your social circle becomes wider than ever.

"Comrades, as you know, the birthday boy has turned 18. He has done something new and innovative to mark his adulthood...." Vivek stopped midway to create the suspense.

"What?" we asked in unison.

"He has created a new blog page titled 'BABES' where he is going to talk only about girls, sex and, of course, boys' *hawas*!" Vivek announced. All the people round the table burst into laughter. The bloody birthday boy gave a smile as if he had achieved an Oscar or a Nobel Prize.

"Mother Fucker, what a name! Good way to mark your 18th birthday!" Rohan remarked.

Next half an hour, we held a full-fledged discussion on porn sites along with the food.

"Rohan and Abhi, we have a counter-strike match this Saturday," Vivek informed us after the meal. Counterstrike, the game is endemic and epidemic. Those who play know why the game is so appealing. For them, it is more than a religion. We four had named our team as 'Slayers'. Except for a few occasions, we always played exceptionally well and were best in the business.

"But this time we have a punt," Naidu quipped with his caveat.

"How much?" I asked.

"Five hundred bucks. So we have to give our best shot," Vivek replied.

"The other team is really good. People say that they are the best in their locality. We expect a good fight," Naidu gave an apprehensive look.

In a game, victory is all that matters. It was not five hundred bucks but our reputation that was at stake. Every regular at cyber café knew about our group and looked up to us. We could not afford to lose the admiration and respect we had earned.

"Don't worry, we will trounce them. Come for the practice tomorrow," said a high-spirited Rohan patt Naidu's head. Rohan was the best player amongst us. His precision and agility made him a threat for the opponents.

Next day our practice lasted four hours. We chalked out a strategy and girded ourselves for the upcoming match. Finally, the D-day arrived. We were supposed to stay overnight at the city café. Though illegal, the practice of staying overnight at cafes is prevalent in Kota. Our predecessors made it a custom and we carried it forward for our posterity. My landlord granted me the permission on the pretext of exam preparations at Vivek's room. Stricter the authority, the more is the tendency to dent it. The law of adolescence! If you happen to live in a hostel, then you learn several ways to win over the warden or the guard, whosoever is stymieing you.

The war started at 11 p.m. The fierce battle between the two wannabe champs continued for many rounds. Unfortunately Slayers lost the war. That was not our day. We underwent a brutal rape. The other team unlike us, played like professionals. One of them walked to us and remarked, "You guys played well. But you lacked coordination. Your keyboard speed did not match our pace. Anyway, you gave us a good fight," his words did nothing to lift our morale.

We returned to our rooms at 7 in the morning. On our way, we discussed a lot about the match and further implications of our loss.

"Abhi, *saale*, you were too slow on the keys. Had you been a little more agile, we could have put up a very good stance," Naidu said with dejection on his face.

I was disheartened with Naidu's remark. I knew it was my fault but the timing of his remark was wrong. I felt that I alone let Slayers down. When I reached my room, I was completely exhausted. I took my cell phone to set an alarm. Two unread messages rested in my inbox. The first one was from Shruti and the other one was from Aditi. I overlooked the first one to jump to the second.

'*Exams over. 2morow test at 10. See u at KCP. Book the tickets. Gud Nite.*'

The message was sent last night. A sudden smile spread on my face. The loser in me turned into a winner.

We went for the matinee show. Being a holiday, the theatre was houseful. Last time I had seen Aditi at KCP, she was distant and with her friends. This time, she was alone and sitting close to me. I could not have asked God for more. Had our mothers not been best friends, we would not have been sitting together. Thank you Mom and Sheetal Aunty! You both made it possible. I thanked them a zillion times.

The movie was an action movie. For most of the time, the thrill, stunts and twists of the movie kept us hooked to the screen.

"So, did you like the movie?" I asked Aditi.

"Yeah, absolutely. It was wonderful. The screenplay was great," she smiled.

"I have an intuition that you are starving. In fact, so am I. Let us go to some restaurant."

"I like that. Smart move!" she giggled and continued. "Aunty was telling me that you were very mischievous and naughty as a child."

"What? Mom called you? What more did she tell about me?"

"Hold on. There is nothing to be worried of. She was just inquiring about you."

"Did she ask you to spy on me?"

She laughed and said, "Why are you being so apprehensive? There is nothing like that. Let us go to the Durbar restaurant

and discuss. It is a nice place."

We took an autorickshaw to the Durbar. Aditi knew more about the city than me. Her choice was really good. The food at the restaurant was delicious; especially the white chicken was very tasty. I ended up licking my fingers.

"So how were your papers?" I should have asked her that question earlier. Talking about studies, and that too with a girl is so stupid and embarrassing.

"School exams were just a formality. The coaching class test was tough but I think I will manage to score well."

"You know, one thing noticeable about you is your mesmerising eyes with beautiful shades of eyelashes. Besides, you are always cheerful."

"Yeah, I know. Everybody says so. So, you tell me how have you been doing at Apex?"

I hated her question. I wanted to know what she thought about me particularly; my appearance.

"Well, things have not been so bright. Initially I was demoted to a lower batch and have been struggling since then," I said in a sad tone.

"Don't worry. Your hard work will pay one day," she put her hand on mine.

O my God! So there is also benefit in performing bad, I thought. She continued keeping her hand for a few seconds and then took it away. All this while, I felt on the ninth cloud.

But the sad part was that there was not an ounce of romance in that touch. The conspirators of my story knew my wants and wishes, so they were spinning the plot in accordance to my expectations. The very foundation of the conspiracy was laid down by my mother and her best friend.

Yummy ice creams followed the mouthwatering food. Later I dropped Aditi at her place. Before going to bed, I got an SMS from her.

Thanks a lot for everything. I completely enjoyed your treat. I owe you one. Gud nite. Take care.'

The SMS was certainly a sign of positive development in my conspiracy. To get a girl, colour the trap with embellishments and cajoleries.

"Rotational mechanics—indeed a hard topic. Students get nightmares while solving the sums. Be attentive throughout all the lectures," Prof. Sen emphatically told the whole class.

Mr Sen had done M-tech from IIT, Delhi and was known as the best teacher of mechanics in the whole institute. Though our batch did not come up to his standard, we got him as a result of rotation of teachers. His moustache never made a curve for he hardly smiled.

"In rotation, a body rotates about an axis. Then there is a centripetal force which is towards the axis…." he kept writing mathematical notations on the blackboard.

Sitting in the third row, I was trying my best to follow him. Unfortunately what was going inside my mind was a real life analogy of rotational mechanics. Aditi being the axis, me being the particle in rotation and love being the centripetal force. To my amusement, both love and centripetal force were inversely proportional to distance. Science and love have so much in common!

"You, blue T-shirt! Stand up."

A stiff voice brought the class to a halt. An annoyed Prof. Sen stood pointing a finger at me. I felt like awaking from a dream.

"Tell me, what is a pseudo force?" he continued in his angry tone.

"It is a kind of force which is, which is applied during rotation…" I stammered while I spoke.

"So here is the Einstein of the class. What is your name?" he interrupted me with a devilish smile.

"Abhi Sharma."

"So Mr Sharma, what is mathematical equivalent of centrifugal force?" he shot another arrow from his quiver.

I knew about centripetal force but this sister force of centripetal was little known to me.

"Sir, I don't know." It was better to say a 'no' rather than to beat about the bush.

"So for the last half an hour I have been teaching hard

and you idiot was absent-minded in the class. How do you even think of getting a seat in IIT? Useless creature! Students like you are just wasting your parents' money. You moron, get out of my class. You are suspended for the whole next week," he poured out all his anger in one breath. His threatening face made me so nervous that I could not even plead for forgiveness. Maybe a sorry would have worked.

All this while, the whole class kept looking at both of us as if we were playing tennis. To them my ouster was a deterrent to not even think of playing with Mr Sen.

Life always has surprises in store. Sometimes it is sweet, sometimes it is too sour to taste.

"Dude! You are screwed. Rotation is the most important topic of physics and Sen is the best at Apex," Vivek remarked.

"I know that. I feel like kicking his ass hard. I was just absent-minded for a few minutes. We are no more school kids. There was no point in suspending me for the whole week. A punishment out of proportion! We pay them more than 60,000 bucks and they bully us like this."

It was now my turn to pour anger. The loser barks only when the winner gets away.

"Oye *Rondu*, forget everything and see this," Naidu put forward a newspaper clipping.

The headline said: '*More than fifty per cent of teenagers in US have sex before 17.*'

"I wish I was born there. Life is super cool there. *Masti, daaru* and *sex*. No worry for grades and enjoy with girls," Naidu commented.

"Shut up. You wannabe Don Juan! Life there is too artificial. There is no love, no trust; only lust. And Indian girls are far better in all respects," Rohan sternly opposed Naidu. The lover boy had the authority on account of his experience with Neha.

"Okay Mr Lover, I agree with you. But what I am saying is that our counterparts in the US have more freedom, more fun and still they rule the planet," Naidu said.

"In India too you have all this. It is just out of reach for a majority of people. And anyway, you can go to a brothel anytime," Vivek advised Naidu.

"Oh! We go to brothel and you have fun with that Bengali chick," Naidu backfired.

"Bengali chick? Who?" I looked at Vivek with bewilderment.

"Well, I was about to tell. Riya Chatterjee, she is in my batch and we have been seeing each other for past one month," he grinned.

"And they have been going on frequent dates," Naidu updated the info. The grin on Vivek's face became wider. After the first batch shuffling, Naidu and Vivek were demoted to a lower batch. Vivek met Riya in that batch. He

kept me and Rohan in the dark.

"You bastard! You did not tell us," I said.

Before Vivek could say anything, Rohan and I got hold of him and there we started–bumps, punches, kicks, everything and anything. Naidu too joined us. It was our style of celebration.

"Please, please, leave me," Vivek pleaded.

"*Haraami*, promise us a treat and we leave you."

"Okay, after the test."

We stopped our unusual celebration. The pain replaced the grin on Vivek's face.

Bengali girls are well known for their beauty. Several successful Bollywood actresses are a testimony to this fact. I had seen several beautiful Bengali girls in my hometown, Jamshedpur. So Vivek falling for her was not that surprising. In our group, Rohan already had a girl; now Vivek got it too. I was still single as far as the relationship status was concerned, but I was too eager to join the lovers' league.

Next morning, when I was taking my habitual tea at Raju's tea-stall, I overheard two boys sitting near. One of them was saying. "You know, yesterday Prof. Sen suspended a student for the whole week. My PG mate was in the same class. The boy was such a dumbo; poor guy."

I felt like slapping the talker. Such things spread like forest fire. Nowadays there is a glamorous term for it—

'breaking news'. That day Abhi Sharma's ouster was the breaking news. Anyway, there was nothing I could have done and ignoring them was the best option.

Our third test came as a surprise. The test was completely objective and questions were relatively easy. Cribbing is easy in such a scenario. Loose invigilation and use of option-symbolic fingers with neighbours catalysed the whole process. Those who had earlier experience of cheating in school, their life flourished. Eventually some of us, including me, paved the way to the upper part of the rank list. A large hue and cry followed the results. Some students who felt cheated by cheating made a complaint to the authority. After much speculation and the shuffling of batches, which was to be done on the basis of that test, was withheld. All four of us had scored remarkably. Had there been shuffling, we four would have been sitting in the top batches.

"Damn it! I wish to kill those complaint-boxes who made this happen," I said. I was frustrated. The only time I performed, they refused to acknowledge.

"But you did not deserve a top batch. You cheated," Aditi said.

"Everyone did it. I was not alone. Who knows whether the ones sitting in the top batch are really sincere and honest?" I backfired at her.

"Okay, Abhi! Keep your temper cool. This is not the end. You still have enough opportunities."

I kept silent.

We were walking by Radha-Krishna temple. For last few days our meetings, or the pseudo-dates as I used to say, became a regular phenomenon. We both liked each other's company. And on account of time spent with her, I could say that though a junior to me, she was wiser than me.

"Let us go to the temple," she suggested. I nodded.

On our way to the temple, she told me about her devout faith in Lord Krishna and Radha.

Was she signalling to something? I kept thinking.

The ambience in the temple was divine and peaceful. Though Aditi was a regular there, I was on my maiden visit. What attracted my attention was the backside of the shrine room. The wall was scribbled all over. The writings were basically wishes made to the God. Some asked for a good rank in IIT, AIEEE or PMT; some asked for a successful love life while others for both.

The one which intrigued me the most said:

'O God! Please bestow me and Anu good ranks in IIT-JEE and take us to the altar as soon as possible—Sanchit'

"Should I write one for us?" I wisecracked. She first read the scribble and then poked me. I smiled and moved forward.

"So Mr Cheater, trying to be oversmart," she tweaked me on my arm as we came out of the temple.

"No, but I am smarter than you," I jerked my hand back.

"Oho! So, do you think that you can get a higher rank than me in IIT-JEE?"

"Well, I don't mind losing to you. I always pray that all your wishes are fulfilled."

"So sweet of you," her eyes gleamed with emotion. Emotion of a different kind!

"Do you know Vivek is dating someone? She is his batchmate."

She knew pretty well about the four of us.

"That is great," she exclaimed.

"She is a Bengali; some Riya Chatterjee."

"Hold on," Aditi interrupted and continued, "Riya Chatterjee from Apex classes, right?"

"Yes," I said.

"O my God, I don't believe this."

"What?"

"She is my room-mate."

"What!" she shocked me with the revelation. Aditi lived in a girls' hostel in Bada Nagar. She never told me about her room-mate.

"Yeah, last year I was in a single room. This year, the warden shifted me with her. Riya is a really nice girl," she further explained.

For the next few seconds, we kept smiling at this fortuitous connection. We both were astonished.

"I should go now. It is getting late," she looked at the watch. It was 7:30 p.m.

"Give me a ring at night."

"Okay."

We bade goodbye to each other. On my way back to the room, I kept thinking about Aditi and Riya. What a strange coincidence? I was completely taken aback by the surreal connection.

"It is really unbelievable," Vivek was completely amused when I told him about Riya and Aditi.

Next Saturday, we four bunked our classes at the Apex Institute. We had planned for a movie with Riya and Aditi. Later we went for a lavish dinner sponsored by Vivek. Riya was a really sweet girl and lived up to her Bengali tag but one could easily say that Aditi was more beautiful of the two. I was proud of the fact.

"Abhi! Aditi told me that your mothers were best friends in college. What about you both?" Riya asked.

"I think Aditi can answer that better." I knew Riya was trying to tease me. So I preferred to throw the ball in Aditi's court. Aditi gave me an 'I-will-kill-you' look and replied, "We are good friends. We met only a few days back, so didn't get much time to spend together."

Smart answer from a beautiful girl!

"You tell me Riya, what good did you find in this simpleton?" I asked, pointing towards Vivek. I retaliated on behalf of both of us.

Everyone on the table except Vivek laughed.

"Well, we both like each other and he has been really nice to me. I think he is not just good, but the best for me."

"O! O!" we all clapped in tandem with shrills for her impeccable answer. All eyes in the restaurant were glued on us. I never saw Vivek so happy.

Who had thought that something like this would happen? Riya, Vivek and Aditi appeared to be pieces of a puzzle that were finally in the bag. Maybe some more pieces were waiting.

That night I sent a SMS to Aditi. It was no joke, no *shayari*, no flirtatious in nature. It was something more.

'What do you think of the question Riya asked in the restaurant?"

She did not reply. Maybe she was asleep or pretended so; maybe she was also thinking about the same question.

Joker's Jottings

Never look at a girl's SMS inbox. The long list of your competitors will make you green with envy. And chemical guys please find a chemical to kill neurotic rodents like Prof. Sen. Each of us has many Sens in our lives. No unwanted material, please!

About mechanics, one which can't be learned, please let's not talk. It simply sucks.

Chapter Six

Pseudo Honeymoon and the Tiff

I could not even learn the basics of rotational mechanics. After a week-long suspension, I resumed attending physics classes. I was now more cautious and tried my best to get a grip on the next topic being taught. What happens to a chain if one of its links becomes weak? The chain becomes frail. The same thing happened with me. Very soon a new teacher replaced Prof. Sen. Unlike Prof. Sen, he treated students nicely but failed at clearing doubts.

Same was the story with chemistry. Our organic chemistry teacher never taught us the concepts but the ways to cram countless theories and reactions. Off the record, there were

hardly two proficient teachers of organic chemistry at Apex Institute. It was nearly impossible for them to look after 50 plus batches. Everybody knew it. The majority suffered.

Mathematics was always the hardest among the three. And with complicated calculus, the situation exacerbated. The real problem haunting the institute was the lack of competent teachers who could incite a zeal and interest in their subjects. The teacher-student ratio was very poor.

The cumulative effects of all these was that I developed a disinterest in classes. I started bunking lectures. There was no point in sitting there and absorbing nothing. I thought better to try for self-study. But most often the self-study ended up in a gaming or movie session at a cyber café or play station. With the exception of Rohan, we three were on the same side of the river. So I never had to worry about company.

Distance always affects relationship. Shruti and I lost the warmth we shared. For several weeks we did not inquire about each other. Our love interests overshadowed the friendship. On the other hand, Aditi and I became chatterboxes over the phone. We used to talk for hours. The telecom companies— Take care of lovebirds very well by providing various apposite plans. Diwali vacations were round the corner. Everyone had booked the tickets. So had Aditi and I. But a few days before the vacation, she changed her mind. She decided to sacrifice celebrations for the preparations. After much thinking, I also cancelled my ticket.

"Mummy, I am not coming home this Diwali. I want to utilise this time for my preparation," I informed her.

My mother lauded my decision as for her it denoted my sincerity and determination. She did not know that I was doing it for Aditi, her best friend's daughter. Two days before the vacation started, I told Aditi about my changed plans. She was astounded.

"Are you crazy? Why are you not going?" she asked.

"Because I want to be with you," I retorted.

"But..."

"Let us plan how to celebrate Diwali and make it stamped on our memories," I interrupted her.

We planned a meet in the evening. There was a peculiar thing about the houses in Kota: either they were magnificently built or they were too congested to distinguish. Ironically the streets followed the same way. At places the roads were far from smooth. The roads in Bada Nagar belonged to that category. Presence of several pigs in some parts was an unsightly addition to the area. Still it was the most popular ghetto of students in the city. I was on my way to Bada Nagar. The roads were crowded with students. A majority of students led a colourless life with no games and fun. Their tedious study schedules gave them no respite. The worst part was that leaving aside some cases, most of them

were dissatisfied with their performance. Hundreds of students led a life of unhappiness and frustration. Overpopulation, peer pressure and cut-throat competition was to blame.

All of a sudden a motorbike halted in front of me. Two persons in their early twenties got off from it.

"Did you tease my sister in front of Modern School?" one of them asked in anger.

I was shocked and confused at this out-of-the blue question.

"No, not at all," I replied. Modern School was on the way to Bada Nagar and barely a few minutes ago I had passed by it. The school was known for girls.

"Come with us. If my sister absolves you, you walk away," the same person said. His long hair and stubble gave him a mafia look.

"Why would I do such a lewd thing? I think you are mistaken," I suggested.

"If you are sane, then why don't you come with us? Once his sister ascertains your innocence, we will drop you wherever you want," the other man said.

I had no idea why they zeroed in on me! There were so many people walking on the road. Anybody could have done that. Why was I being made a suspect? Disagreeing with them would create further suspicion and troubles. As a result I had to agree. Riding triple seat on a two-wheeler was an offence. Rules? Who cares? Rules are like mules. Everybody loves to make a mockery of them. The two men sandwiched me on the bike.

"Where are we going?" I asked.

"To my house," the rider said.

"And where is it?"

"Two kilometers from here."

I had no clue that I had opened a Pandora's box by allowing myself to go with those two guys until the bike stopped on a deserted road. It was already dark and there were no streetlights. The person sitting behind me got down and asked me to do the same. To my shock, the rider took out a knife and butt it against my navel. I felt the pointed tip pinching my stomach.

"You rascal, take out everything you have or I am going to tear your stomach apart," he said. He pressed the knife against my stomach. I shrieked. The other man standing behind me caught my neck. I had never been in such a situation and from my experience I can say that no matter how clever and sharp you are, your brain gets numb and stops thinking. Everything was like a bolt from the blue. I was terrorised and my eyes were panicky. I gave away everything—wallet, cell-phone, watch and a gold chain. They slammed me hard in the stomach and went away. The jab was very powerful. I stooped, disabling myself from seeing the number plate. I walked back to Jaiswal villa with pain in the stomach, anger in blood and helplessness in eyes.

"It was really sad. I was worried the whole night. Your phone was also switched off," Aditi said.

"Yeah, I know. They took it away. I wish I had a gun to shoot the heads of those bloody hoodlums."

"But you should not have gone with them," she commented.

"I know I acted foolish. Actually they appeared genuine so I trusted them. Fucking bastards," I let the anger out.

"Hey, don't use such words in the temple premises," she warned.

We were sitting in the lawn of Radhe-Krishna temple. Aditi thought that visiting the temple would help in my reconciliation.

"Did you register an FIR?"

"Yeah, in the morning. I went with Jaiswal Uncle."

"Mummy was asking about you." The news of the unfortunate incident spread like forest fire. It was better that my phone was gone, otherwise numerous calls and consolations would have pissed me off. My parents were so disturbed on hearing the news that they suggested that I return to Jamshedpur. But there was no logic in their advice. Such incidents occur every day in our country. It was my first happenstance with real India.

We stayed for an hour in the temple. Talking to Aditi made me feel better. Thereafter I went to Vivek's room. Like everyone else, they too were sad for me.

"So here is your phone," Naidu gave me a handset. I had asked him in the morning to arrange for one.

"You know, we can find out those bastards," Vivek said.

I gave him a startled look and asked, "How?" I was eager to know.

"Actually they sell those stolen items in Chor Bazaar. If we go there and spend some time and money, then we can get clues about them. Besides, Chor Bazaar is a weekly event which gets operational in the wee hours of Wednesday. It will be easy for us."

"Probability of succeeding is very less, so it is better that you forget about the incident," Naidu advised. "Cheer up and have a blast this Diwali,"

I nodded. It was better to forget what had happened rather than brooding about it.

"When are you guys leaving?" I asked.

"Tomorrow," Vivek said.

Almost everyone was leaving the city the same day. Next evening, I went to the railway station to see off Vivek and Naidu. Rohan had already left for Bhillai in the afternoon. The whole platform was brimming with the fervour of festivity. Hundreds of students were waiting for their

respective trains. Some of them were bellowing, some were struggling with their luggage while others were loitering near gangs of girls. There was a joy of escapism on everyone's face.

"*Phodu*! *Phodu*! Party! Party!" Flocks of students on the opposite platform yelled in unison. It catapulted a shout spree, which was mainly an illogical combination of words. The situation at the junction got funny and frolicsome until the railway police went into action. Their sticks brought the chaos to a halt. Waiting for a train is always a humdrum experience but things were different then.

All this while, Vivek was busy exchanging last minute endearing words with Riya. Her train was about to depart in a few minutes. They were behaving too filmy and melodramatic. I kept myself engaged with Aditi, who was there to see off Riya. Half an hour later, the train bound for New Delhi arrived. All the travellers moved to take their seats.

"You both take care and stay in touch," I said to Vivek and Naidu.

"And you motherfucker, have fun with Aditi," Naidu whispered in my ear. The siren blew and their train sped up to leave the platform. Seeing off is a cumbersome task.

"So what are we doing tomorrow?" I asked Aditi.

"First, let us take an autorickshaw. I am getting late," she said.

"Have you ever been to Chambal Garden?"

"Yes. It is a nice place to hang out. I have been there a few times."

"Then take me around there."

"Smart enough. Eh?"

"I am only asking for a favour."

"First, treat me to a movie," she giggled.

I nodded. Why would I refuse?

The spirit of Kota is in the thousands of inhabitants who come from various parts of the country with dreams and hope. The city serves as a springboard for them. The axle of the city's economy is the education industry. The city is incomplete without students. When I returned to my room, all my PG mates had gone. There was a different type of silence all around, which spoke of the absence of vivacity.

Chambal Garden was not a big park but its picturesque greenery and charm made it a desirable place for everyone. The gently flowing Chambal added glam quotient to it. There was a time when Chambal was synonymous with bandits and though it has transformed itself into a new *avatar*, still its repute remains blotted.

We chose to sit on a bench near the bank. The crescent moon was smiling in the distant sky. The river gleamed with the reflection of lights on its banks. Diwali's new moon was to come in three days.

"Nice song, isn't it?" Aditi said.

The same Punjabi song *'Kala kauwa kaat khayega…'* was being played at some nearby *pandal.*

"Huh! People here seem to be crazy for this song. They are never fed up listening to it," I showed my disinclination for the song. She gave back a grin. The cold breeze kept ruffling her hair. Some locks were displaced to her forehead, but she didn't move them back. She knew that she looked even more beautiful with that.

"I love sitting like this. The ambience is so appealing," she remarked.

"And I love throwing stones in the river," I continued to create ripples.

"I like it too."

I slid my right hand into my pocket and took out a colour used paper which smelt of rose.

"Aditi, this is for you," I held it towards her.

"What is it?" she asked.

"You better see yourself."

There was enough light to read. Written on the paper was:

I knew, one day I would meet you,

For you were always in my dreams and thoughts.

Sometimes you were the angel, sometimes you were the princess.

Sometimes you were holding my hands, sometimes you were

caressing me.

Slowly and swiftly every night passed like that.

Every time it rained, I missed you.

Every dusk I yearned for you.

Every Valentine's I was alone.

Every time I saw Taj Mahal, I thought if I could be there with you

I always wondered wherever you were, whether you felt the same way or not.

Love is blind, love is mad, love has wings.

But for me love is you.

Now the long wait has come to an end

For, you are in front of my eyes.

Now I can touch you, I can talk to you

Without the obnoxious alarm disturbing me.

Now I can be with you, forever and ever.

O my angel! You are the spring of my life

I wish there was no summer.

Hold me and embrace me like never,

For I want to be with you, forever and ever.

A spark of affection appeared in her eyes as she finished reading. She looked at me and said, "For me? How sweet!" Her eyes were moist. It was all quiet outside, but inside both of us was going through a gust. I moved closer to her and touched her hands. They were cold. I took her in my arms. She reclined on my chest and shoulders. That moment I felt a sense of completeness. I kissed on her cheek and she reciprocated.

"I love you," she finally said. Wow! We were in love. Who says that words don't have magic? Just put them in the right order and see. Write a few lines for a girl you hanker after and you will score. I took Aditi to the Chambal's shore. I rounded her neck with my hand. She put her on my waist.

"Look into my eyes," I said. "Do you see enormous love for you?"

She fluttered her eyelids. Her eyes were strikingly captivating. We were close, close enough to be treated as one. Tons of romance spilled out of me.

"You know, I was mad for you since the day I saw you," I said and kissed on her forehead. "Look, the river, the moon and the stars are revelling at the birth of our love," I pointed towards the distant sky and neighbour Chambal.

"I am so glad to have you. Love is so contagious." This time she kissed on my forehead, smiled back and continued, "Don't stop. Keep saying lovely things. I love it."

She held me tightly. The grip grew stronger as I blabbed. Emotions kept us going and we enjoyed every moment in love's oblivion.

I could never forget that evening in Chambal Garden.

The warmth of my first hug and the magic of the first kiss always remained afresh in memory.

"Happy Diwali. May Goddess Lakshmi shower blessings on you," I wished Aditi in the early morning.

"Same to you. Love you."

"Me too."

Celebrations are always incomplete without the family. On the day of Diwali, we both missed our families but we made up with each other. I believe that is what love stands for. We enjoyed our time together. I was very happy. I wanted Aditi and finally had got her. The conspiracy succeeded. Next five days we spent every possible moment together. We talked, we ate, we laughed and we opened up every dark secret of ours.

"Shame! Shame! What would I say to my friends that my boyfriend was in the habit of bed-wetting?" she teased me.

"But I did not stutter as a child and said, helicopter.... helichopcher," I wisecracked.

"Shut up."

"I am a better leg-puller. Don't mess with me," I warned her.

Our pseudo-honeymoon minus nights came to an end with the arrival of students and commencement of classes. When I told Vivek, Naidu and Rohan about what had happened in Chambal Garden, they treated me the way they

treated Vivek. It really hurts when somebody kicks your ass hard. Though their home-made snacks compensated for the painful kicks, I had to apply ointment. With each passing day, the mess food made me yearn more and more for home-cooked dishes. The food there was so unsavoury that in last four months, I had switched over three messes. Alas! There was little improvement in taste.

We planned a pyjama party at Rohan's place to celebrate a belated Diwali. His landlords were out of the city so we had no problems in bringing beer cans and playing loud music.

"So, how is Neha?" I asked Rohan.

"She is absolutely fine. I told her about you guys. She was really eager to meet you all," his face said that he was missing his girlfriend.

"Naidu, why don't you search a girl for yourself? I mean now you are the only single one amongst us," Vivek teased him.

It was not that Naidu had never tried his luck with any girl but the fact was that he was neither good nor his fate favoured him. A few months ago an interesting thing had happened in his life. Naidu was obsessed with Smriti, a girl in his batch who was well known among guys for her deep neckline tops. He always used to take a seat behind Smriti during a lecture in a bid to see her ass crack. Thanks to Smriti's see-my-curvy-hips jeans, Naidu enjoyed voyeurism.

Things started really well between them when he started hanging out with Smriti. He did everything to impress her, treating her at posh restaurants, taking her to movie halls, buying costly gifts for her and taking care of every small things in her life. The process continued till Rakhi, the ill-fated day when Smriti offered a *rakhi* to him with the most dreaded title of *bhai*. All dreams shattered for Naidu that day. Back at room, he broke glasses, buckets and ravaged his study desk. That was a perfect case of KLPD.

"Do I look like a fucking idiot? Making a girlfriend. Those bloody blandishments, squandering money, wasting precious time. This is not my cup of tea. It is better to buy sex rather than beating about the bush like that," Naidu said disapprovingly. Getting a girl is like an achievement and he was far from that. So he didn't like Vivek's question at all.

"You poor turd. Why don't you accept that you are not straight?" I gave a diabolical smile. Vivek and Rohan burst into laughter.

"You asshole! Do I need to fuck your girlfriend to prove my sexual orientation?"

"What? What did you say?" I was enraged. I caught hold of his collar. The situation got tense and before any physical assault started, Rohan and Vivek held us back.

"You bastard! Dare you say anything about Aditi and I will take your balls out," I was offended. I had a reason to be angry. I loved Aditi and was possessive of her. How could I tolerate any bad word about her? I slammed the door hard and walked out of the room sulkily. What started as a light-hearted leg-pulling session ended in an unfortunate fight between me and Naidu. Later, Vivek tried hard to convince me but I did not mellow. The same was the case with Naidu.

"It is really sad. You two were good friends," Aditi remarked.

"I know it. It just happened. I still don't understand why did he say like that?"

"Anyway, there is a bad news for you. Next week I have to attend classes in the school; got some stuff related to pre-boards to do. So no dating and going out."

"From when?"

"Day after tomorrow."

Schooling at Kota was a bit different from elsewhere. Rules were too flexible and the school authority worked in tandem with coaching institutes. There was no need to attend classes daily. No need to worry for attendance. You cannot find a better place than Kota for higher secondary education. Everything was just too perfect.

"From next month onwards an All India Test Series will start. We expect some fifty thousand students to appear in it. So get yourself well prepared. Remember, next few months are going to be very crucial for you. Don't let yourselves and your parents down," the maths teacher announced in the class. As soon as he left the class, a hubbub followed. Everyone started sharing words with his or her neighbour. I could see everyone masquerading. Every single person was jealous of the other and nobody wanted to be left behind in the race. These days, a psychological war among competitors acts as a virtual prelude to the real battle. It happened everywhere—in mess, in classes, in hostels; it was all pervading.

"Do you know, people say that if you secure a rank under two thousand in this All India Test, then your selection in IIT is definite." my bespectacled neighbour told me. I nodded as if I knew it. Rumours are a part of competition.

Joker's Jottings

Honeymoon is such a tempting and sweet affair! Human race owes its existence to it!

Falling in love! Wow! It's a wonderful experience. When I say so, I mean it. Try it. There is nothing sweeter than that. KLPD! What to say? A guy's prerogative! Victim? Beware of that.

Chapter Seven

Jalebis & The Moron's Lesson

"Good morning, Aditi."

She turned back to find herself dumbfounded. "You!" she almost screamed.

"Surprised?"

"Absolutely," she replied.

"Well you look sexy in skirt," I remarked. She poked me for the comment. It was 7'o clock in the morning and she had the least idea that I could come to Bada Nagar to surprise her. A bunch of girls standing nearby were watchful of us. Aditi was fully clad in her school uniform, waiting for the school bus to arrive.

"Let us go by an autorickshaw. We can spend some time together," I suggested.

The offer was too tempting for her. Aditi studied at Global Academy, the school where Jaiswal Uncle's children also studied. The school was far from Bada Nagar. We took an autorickshaw. It was half an hour journey by auto.

"Thanks for coming. I am really elated," she took my hand and started caressing it.

"Yeah, I know," I pulled my hand back and kept it on her thighs and fiddled. Her luscious legs kept my eyes engaged.

"Stop it," she pinched me on arm.

"I wish, I could take it off," I said, pointing toward the skirt. She pinched me harder. We kept on playing naughty till we reached the destination. She got off the auto and said, "I will wait for you at 2:00 p.m," I nodded. She waved her hand and proceeded towards the school gate. What started as an exercise to fawn Aditi became a habit. Escorting her to the school and then back to her hostel became a daily chore. For the whole week I kept bunking my classes at Apex. No records of attendance were maintained, so there was no big deal in that. Academic loss, who cares? Love is blind.

When Rohan came to know about this, he was very censorious.

"Are you crazy? Why are you bunking so many lectures? At least attend the lectures. You can meet Aditi in free time,"

he reprimanded.

But I was deaf to his words. Love is deaf as well. Meanwhile one day in school, Nancy, the ten-year old daughter of Jaiswal Uncle saw me with Aditi. She passed me an I-caught-you-*bhaiya* smile.

It took half a dozen chocolates to get an assurance from her that she will not tell anyone about the incident. Kids these days are clever and more demanding. On Saturday, while coming back from school, Aditi and I went to Hariyali. Hariyali was an open restaurant situated in the suburb of Kota. The place was too big for the two of us. We huddled together in a corner which was covered with lush greenery on three sides.

"Nice place, na," I said. My hands played on her waist.

"You know, I never thought that I would fall in love. My career and academics always took a priority but then, you came and it happened," she said. She kept her head on my shoulder. Things were getting closer.

"For me it was love at first sight. The moment I saw you in the movie theatre, I was smitten by you. It was written in our destiny. I was the Mr Right for you," my hands fondled her hair. They were silky and smooth.

"But you came so late in my life. You know, in last one-and-a-half year I have got more than ten proposals. Alas! Nobody could impress me like you did," she giggled.

"Don't feel so proud of yourself. Blame it on the poor sex ratio of our country. By the way, I also got a few proposals in school but I rejected all of them," I did get them when I was in XI class. Though I flirted with a few, I never committed to anyone.

"But we have to focus on our careers and make sure that our relationship does not affect it."

"I don't care for anything else. I am in love with you and I know that I cannot live a single moment without you." An adrenalin rush was palpable in my tone.

"I love you too. I think we make a great pair. You know, a girl always wants some guy in her life who loves her, who does crazy things for her, gives her the topmost priority and cares for her. For me, you are the one. I feel lucky to have you. Just promise me that we will remain together forever. I don't want to lose you," her hands played with my buttons. It was tickling the testosterone inside me.

"Well, thanks for being so sweet. Don't worry, we are lovers forever. But I have a complaint; I never got any surprises from you. Besides you were." All of a sudden she put her lips on mine. They were soft, softer than her cheeks. Our tongues crawled into each other's mouth. Our eyes closed. Every action was spontaneous. Our first smooch! Least expected but well arrived. The best part of kissing is that you feel a tinge of eternal happiness, something of which

neo-spiritual gurus talk about in their discourse. They should also preach and encourage people to kiss their lovers. Kiss is an expression of love, the best one. Your heart never feels as happy as when you kiss. Those who are deprived, pray to God, very soon you may taste it.

That day we smooched a few times, the longest being about a minute long. Once the ice is broken, you no longer float, but swim. On the return journey, my hands kept playing inside her shirt. I had never enjoyed so much on an auto ride.

As soon as I reached my room, I got a call from Vivek asking me to come to his room. He sounded anxious and agitated.

"What's the matter? Why are you guys look so worried?" I asked. Everyone in the room was sitting with tense looks. It clearly spoken of some trouble.

"There is a problem. A big one," Vivek replied.

"What problem?"

"The problem is Anurag Thakur. He is after Riya and has been threatening Vivek repeatedly for the last two days," Rohan explained the scene for me. Naidu was also there but he preferred to be silent since we were not on speaking terms. He always derived pleasure in explaining things. A chatterbox, he was.

"Give him a thrashing and he will learn his lesson," I said.

"No, here lies the real problem. Anurag is a local boy and he has good contacts with the hoodlums here. He has threatened to come tomorrow with his friends," Vivek expounded the gravity of matter.

"Why don't you report the matter to the police?" Rohan suggested.

"Are you mad? If we tell the police, then Vivek and Riya's relation will come to limelight. There will be a possibility of mudslinging and disclosure to their parents. It is a suicidal step," I censored Rohan's suggestion.

Everyone was satisfied with my stand. They all nodded.

"Did Riya know about this?" I asked.

"Yes. She is also freaked out by Anurag's numerous calls. In fact, yesterday the bastard stalked her on the way to Apex," an infuriated Vivek said. I myself was a victim of local hooliganism, so my sympathy lay completely with Vivek. Touch a guy's girl and he turns into a raging bull.

"Such people should be castrated and put behind the bars," I said and resumed after a short pause, "Don't worry, I have a solution."

"What?" Vivek gave a quizzical look.

"Raghu *bhaiya*. He too is a local. His maternal uncle is an MLA. Besides, he is a reputed bad boy of this area. I know him well and he is the one who can help us," I explained.

I first met Raghu *bhaiya* at Raju's tea-stall. Like me, he

was a regular there. We were on pretty friendly terms. One basic rule of life is that keep all types of people in your social circle. It is always in your best interest.

I dialled Raghu *bhaiya's* number. "Hello *bhaiya*. Abhi here. Actually I am in a problem. It is urgent. Need your help," I said.

After a small conversation I hung up with a smile on my face.

"The problem is solved. He has asked us to meet him early in the morning at Gol Chowk. He was doing something important in a brothel," I announced. Everybody took a deep sigh of relief.

Gol Chowk was a busy market near Bada Nagar. The best thing about the market was that there were dozens of stalls which served *poha*, *jalebis* and tea for students in the wee hours. Students who studied for the whole night visited stalls as early as four in the morning. In Kota, everything was done to ensure a better study environment for students. The organisational behaviour of the education industry is so amazing that the management guys should make a case study on that. Every small piece is in its right place.

We four reached Gol Chowk at 4:30 a.m. The morning *mela* was already in full swing. The whole area was teeming with students. There was a pleasing hullabaloo all around. We had been a number of times to Gol Chowk to eat *poha*, *jalebis* in the wee hours. *Poha* is a special Indian snack made of beaten rice and it was the national food for thousands of students living in Kota. I located Raghu *bhaiya* sitting behind a stall. He was with his friends. People like Raghu are always accompanied by followers who are nothing but poor sycophants.

"Hi, *bhaiya*," I greeted him. I introduced Vivek, Rohan and Naidu to him.

"So, what is the matter? You four look so worried."

"I told you over the phone about that guy, Anurag Thakur. He has intimidated Vivek. He has also been stalking Vivek's girlfriend. He is a local boy and has threatened to come tomorrow with his friends," I said.

"Where does he live?' he asked.

"We don't know. All we have is his contact number," I replied.

"These kinds of people are nothing but pretentious pests. *Saala haraami*. The motherfucker thinks that he is the boss of the city. You know me well. Believe me; I am going to screw this asshole," he said. The way he spoke, we felt that half of the work was done.

"You guys don't worry. I will fix it today itself. Have cigarettes," he offered the packet to us. Except Rohan, all of us were habituated to smoking. The cigarette was of a premium brand, the one which everyone cannot afford.

Some smokers are very choosy and selective about their brand. Raghu *bhaiya* was one of them.

"Bhaiya, I think we will leave now," I said.

"Okay. Enjoy your time and if any problem comes, do come to me."

"Thanks a lot, *bhaiya*." Vivek's eyes brimmed with gratitude.

"No, Bro. Abhi is my own man and you are his friend. Your enemy is my enemy. If that asshole calls you again, just say that you are a relative of Raghu *bhai*," he patted Vivek's shoulders.

Raghu *bhaiya's* assurance brought a sense of security and relief on our faces. We took our way back to Gyan Vihar.

"Let us give this good news to Riya," I nudged Vivek on the way.

"But she must be sleeping now," he said.

"Oh! Come on. Let us go to her hostel and surprise her."

"Okay," the idea finally appealed to him. We bade goodbye to Rohan and Naidu and walked toward Bada Nagar. We bought one kilogram *jalebis* and divided it in two parts.

"Hi, Shyam *bhaiya*. How are you?" I greeted.

"What a surprise! I am fine. Is everything okay?" he asked. Shyam Singh was the night-guard of the hostel where Aditi and Riya lived. In day shift, the duty was assigned to Ram Singh, his brother. Vivek and I had developed pretty good ties with both of them. On account of small favours we did for them, they offered their loyalty to us. The last one was arranging a second-hand camera-phone at a very reasonable price. An inevitable truth of boys' life is that if their girlfriends live in a hostel, then they ought to have the guards on their side. The guards have the keys to success. Shyam *bhaiya* knew very well about our love interests.

"*Bhaiya*, we thought that you would be hungry so we brought this for you," I handed a plastic bag containing *jalebis* to him.

"We want to meet Riya for a few minutes. We have brought *jalebis* for her too. If you please..."

"Okay, okay. Wait for a minute," shyam Singh interrupted Vivek.

"And Aditi too," I shouted. He turned back and signalled a 'yes'.

Shyam Singh belonged to a village in eastern Uttar Pradesh. At the age of twenty, he eloped with his childhood sweetheart and since then he had been living at Kota. This was the primary reason for his fellow feeling for us.

When Vivek told Riya the whole thing, her face shone with joy. I could see that from a nearby corner where Aditi and I were standing.

"Why the hell have you come now?" Aditi's voice was sleepy. She looked both astonished and annoyed.

"Your voice is so cute and you look glamorous in this pink night-suit," I remarked.

She smiled. A yawn followed the smile.

"Don't be so filmy. Why did you take so much of risk?" the Hitler in her asked.

"Well, I have something important to tell you. Apart from that, I have brought *jalebis* for you," I gave the plastic bag to her.

"Thanks a lot. But there was no need to disturb my sleep for these *jalebis*. Now tell the important thing."

"The important thing is....that....I love you," I grinned.

"O! It is really very important," she tweaked my cheek and commented.

"So, anything important you want to say?" I asked.

"Yes, and that is, I hate you, my filmy hero. Now go back before the warden finds you."

"Okay, Boss." The meeting was too short but sweet. She walked inside the hostel with *jalebis*.

"So what was Riya's reaction?" I asked Vivek.

"She was extremely happy. Thank you, Abhi. It is all possible because of you. I am obliged to you," Vivek's words touched the strings of my heart.

"Come on, man. Don't be so emotional. We are friends and I did what I was supposed to do." Vivek embraced me. I felt the warmth of our friendship. We Indians love melodrama. Don't we?

One day later Vivek got a message from Anurag Thakur.

'Hey Dude! Sorry for creating trouble. Wish you & Riya a happy future ahead.'

Later we came to know that Raghu *bhaiya* ruptured Anurag's both legs. The moron finally learnt the lesson.

Joker's Jottings

Skirts lead to scandals. Don't they? Ban it or allow scandals.

And make yourself a well-known personality in the girls' hostel guards' association. It's cliché but effective. Guard bhaiya *ki jai ho!*

Chapter Eight

The Blast, the Hero and Two Devils

"I never knew that you were so good a troubleshooter," Aditi remarked.

"Well, you are lucky that you have got a guy like me. Multi-talented!" I shrugged my collar.

"O really!" she gave a gentle jab on my chest. "But don't be too involved with these bad boys. You may be in big trouble some day."

"Oh! Don't worry. I am smart enough," I boasted.

There cannot be a better thing than a girl in anyone's life. Romantic, caring, bossy, emotional; she can take all the forms. Aditi loved and cared for me madly. I was her Kohinoor.

"By the way, Riya was heaping loads of praise on you. I feel delighted on hearing good stuff about you," she smiled.

"I am like that. Praiseworthy. Isn't it?"

"Yeah," she took a deep breath and continued, "but right now, I am starving. Let us go to the Durbar."

"No. I am bored of that place. Let us go to Convenio this time. I have heard that some of its dishes are mouth-watcring."

Eating out was like a celebration in Kota. It gave an escape from the usually tasteless food of the mess. But affordability was always a big question. Convenio was certainly smaller than the Durbar but its exterior was intricately decorated.

"It looks nice," Aditi commented. We entered the restaurant with glued hands and hearts. We chose to sit in a corner. As I was about to take a seat, I heard a familiar voice, "Abhi!" I turned around to find the source of the sound. What I saw made me surprised as well as shocked. Jaiswal Uncle and his family members were sitting in the distant corner. I almost froze. He must have seen me holding Aditi's hands, I thought. I was caught red-handed. My hunger vanished like a candle in the wind. I walked towards their table. Every step I took was like walking on a sword. I tried hard to smile but I failed.

"Hi!" I said fumblingly.

"What a surprise! Any problem with the mess?" Mrs Jaiswal asked.

All eyes looked at me. I knew they wanted to know something else.

"No, the mess is okay. Actually I came with my friend. Today is her birthday. So we thought to eat out," I said and pointed towards Aditi. I was caught in a nasty situation and there was no time to frame better lies.

"What's her name?" he asked.

"Aditi," I replied.

"Why don't you both join us? We would be really happy to have you here," Jaiswal Uncle had given us an invitation. What do I say? How do I refuse? And if I don't, it could be a disaster. I thought.

"Call her here," Mrs Jaiswal said. I had no other choice. I obeyed. We joined them on the table. Everybody wished her a happy birthday. She was surprised by their gesture but understood everything within seconds. Thankfully, she was smart enough, otherwise I would have been caught naked. We ordered the food. Thieves were dining with the police.

"Papa, I have seen Abhi *bhaiya* with this girl in my school." The unexpected revelation came from Nancy, Jaiswal Uncle's daughter. Bad luck continued for me. Everybody looked at me, demanding an explanation. There was an uncomfortable silence. Aditi's face showed uneasiness.

"Actually my coaching teacher is the vice-principal of Global Academy. I had some doubts, so he asked me to come there. Fortunately I met Aditi there," I lied. Thank God! My reflexes were great. Everybody looked satisfied. Love and lies are interconnected. A good lover is always a good liar.

For the next half an hour the food kept us busy. I silently prayed to God not to worsen the situation further. The food was good but I could not relish it properly.

"Uncle, I need to drop Aditi back at her hostel. I think we will now leave," I said humbly.

"You can come with us by car. There is enough space," Mrs Jaiswal suggested.

I looked at Jaiswal Uncle. My eyes begged for the permission to go away.

"Okay, if you are fine with an autorickshaw, then you may proceed." He was very kind.

"Goodnight and thanks a lot for the food," I said and walked briskly with Aditi towards the exit.

"This was the worst dinner of my life. Why the hell did we go there? I wish we had gone to the Durbar. Wrong place, wrong time and wrong people," I vented my frustration.

"For the whole time, your face was like a pumpkin. I could hardly stop my smile," she teased.

"Stop it, Aditi. This is no joke. You don't understand the gravity of this matter. What if Jaiswal Uncle calls my father?

And imagine our parents' fury if they come to know about our relationship," I was tense.

"It is a complete disaster then," Aditi sounded serious now. She now understood how things could go off the track.

"Let us pray and hope for the best. We have to be brave," I took her hands and kissed them. The evening was certainly not a pleasant one. Perhaps God was punishing me for what happened with Anurag, I thought.

That night Jaiswal Uncle came to my room. I pretty much expected it.

"Do you love that girl?" he asked.

"Yes," I tried to avoid his eyes.

He smiled, certainly to make me feel comfortable.

"But Uncle, please don't tell my parents about it," I pleaded.

"Don't worry, I will not. I don't have a say in your personal matters. You are prudent enough to understand that next few months are critical for your career. I hope you won't let your love life affect your career. If it impairs, then it is not love. Do well and nobody would have a problem with your girlfriend," he talked like a friend. I liked his approach. It was the way I wanted.

"Thanks for being a good friend. I would take care of that."

"By the way, Aditi is a nice girl. You two look good

together," he remarked before leaving the room. I smiled. His visit worked as a panacea for my apprehensions. Good people are still there on this earth. You find them only if you are in a trouble.

"So, are you guys working hard?" Prof. Gupta asked the class.

"Noooooo," the whole class screamed. There was still enough energy left even after an hour long torturing lecture on calculus. Why didn't our forefathers keep things simple and straight in academics? Some topics are so hard that you reach the nadir of frustration while learning them. And even if you succeed in grasping them, you still fail at solving sums. Calculus was the perfect example.

"Well, if you are not serious, then God knows what will happen with you when the results are out? Do you know that 40 students fight for a single seat in IIT? So, mathematically I can say that only two of you will make it to IIT. What about the rest?"

The whole class went silent. There was a time when our elders talked of hope, success, happiness and motivation in a positive way. Nowadays they talk only about the fear of failure. They terrorise us with the fear of darkness. Such teachers and parents are at large. A sun never rises from the fear of darkness.

"Study more than 12 hours a day and next year you will

be at some IIT. When I was of your age, I used to toil 14 hours daily and it was by virtue of my hard work that I secured an All India Rank 430," Mr Gupta continued.

The whole class clapped. He returned back a victorious smile.

"But, sir, at times we work very hard and we do not get the desired results. It makes us depressed and gives a low self-esteem. What should we do?" Somebody from the back benches shot the question.

"I think there is a fault in the way you approach. Make it right and you will get what you want. If anyone has such problems, then feel free to talk to me. Anyway, I will leave now."

"Sir, we have heard that you sing exceptionally well. We want to hear a song from you," a girl from the front row demanded. It is hard to say 'no' to a pretty girl. Prof. Gupta sang an oldie. He was a good singer. His voice resembled Kishore Kumar. When he finished singing, we started shouting. "Once more, *Phodu*! Once more, *Phodu*!" He left the class with exaltation on his face.

When I told Aditi about what had happened between me and Jaiswal Uncle she retorted.

"Well, this time you should be thankful to God that you got a girl like me. It was my congeniality and demure behaviour that saved your ass."

Though that was an exaggeration, it was not all false. I nodded.

"So you owe me a favour," she chuckled.

I was ordered to complete her lab records. It took me five hours to write 15 experiments along with convoluted diagrams which really freaked me out. Sometimes you have to make sacrifices. There is no escape. Hail girl power!

Next morning a knock disturbed my sleep. I opened the door to find Naidu standing there. After that verbal abuse, we never talked a word to each other and all of a sudden he appeared in front of me.

"I am really sorry about that day. I was a bit aggressive and I should not have said like that," he apologised. His eyes were effusive. He looked at me for a response.

"I am also sorry for what happened." We shook hands and hugged each other. All that it takes to forget such silly fights is a gentle 'sorry'. But the problem lies with our ego which makes us reticent for that.

"And dude, I heard about that Convenio incident. You were nearly screwed. A narrow escape," he said.

"Yes, it was, but thankfully everything got fixed in the end. My landlord is a really nice and easy-going person," I smiled. The sordid sulk between me and Naidu was broken by the surreal reconciliation. Still there was some discomfort in the air.

"Tonight, it is Arsenal versus Manchester United, the final I have made arrangements at the city café. The match starts at 11 p.m.," Naidu said.

"I know, ManU is going to trounce Arsenal."

"Dude, I bet this is not going to happen this time," he showed me the middle finger.

We were crazy for football but always were on opposite sides. He loved France, while I was an ardent supporter of Germany. While Man-U was my favourite, he was a die-hard supporter of Arsenal.

"Okay, then the punt is on. The one who loses owes a treat at Punjabi *dhaba*," I said.

"Sure, see you in City Café."

"Listen, I forgot to congratulate you. You joined my league by getting a week's suspension from the class," I said. He smiled and left the room.

Naidu was given detention for he had not done the assignments in chemistry. His chemistry teacher was nothing less than a devil. *Ravana*—that was what students called him. Though a large chunk of students usually failed to complete out-of-proportion assignments, Ravana made Naidu a scapegoat to set a deterrent. Everybody cannot work like a machine.

The match started at the scheduled time. There were around 30 students in the café. Football has only a few takers in India. The thrill of the match pepped all of us. The vibe was so lively that we felt like sitting in the stadium. The crowd was bifurcated, each supporting their gods. Action continued.

"Voila! Whooooo," we screamed. Ronaldo had scored a goal. In the twenty-ninth minute of the game, Man-U took the lead. We started throwing beer cans and caps at the gloomy Arsenal fans. They were disheartened. They pretty well knew that even the best goalie on Earth could not have stopped that goal. A few minutes before half time, my phone rang. I thought it was Aditi as it was our usual gossip time. The more you talk in love the happier and more satisfied you feel. But my phone flashed the name of Sushmita Aunty. It was 11:40 p.m. Why would she call me so late at night? I thought.

"Hi Aunty! How are you?" Sushmita Aunty was Shruti's mother. She was a very nice person and a good cook. I loved her dishes. An absolute delight to eat!

"Hi, Abhi..." she was crying. Her voice choked.

"What happened, Aunty? Why are you crying? Is everything okay?" I felt strange.

What I heard in the next two minutes turned my world upside down. Shocking, devastating and terrible. The whole world fell apart for her as well as me. That evening there had been a blast in Delhi. Unfortunately Shruti had got injured

badly in the blast. She was rushed to AIIMS. The incident happened around 8 p.m. My hands were wet, so were my cheeks. Tears cascaded from my eyes. I walked out of the City Café. That was a full stop to my celebration. My best friend was struggling for her life in the ICU. I felt like blowing away those heinous terrorists who orchestrated the blast. For the first time in my life I felt the ripple of the atrocities of terrorism.

Next morning I took a train to Delhi. The journey took six long, anxious hours. All this while, my heart kept weeping. My elder brother, Aman, had been a student at AIIMS, so I had been to the place before. When I reached there, I met Shruti's parents. They had flown down early in the morning. The situation was grim. Sushmita Aunty embraced me. My shoulders shared the moistness of her cheeks. How would a mother feel if her only child is struggling for life?

"How is she now?" I asked her.

"Doctors have asked to wait for another 12 hours. If she regains consciousness, then she survives, or else ....." Vijay Uncle choked. He was Shruti's father and a renowned surgeon in Jamshedpur. His face was dull with pain but he didn't let it come out in his voice; rather, he sounded brave.

"Everything is going to be fine. Isn't it?" I wanted to know the details.

"We hope so. She is recovering fast but the damage is extensive," he said.

I was very anxious to see Shruti, but given that she was in the ICU, none of us could meet her. We had not seen each other since she had left Jamshedpur for her admission in Delhi University. And the last time we talked was a month ago. We both got busy in our love lives. I did not see any guy around, so I assumed that Prateek, her boyfriend, was not present. Maybe he does not know about the accident, I thought.

We waited in the hospital for the whole night. Nobody could sleep. All night we kept praying to God. Most of the time, Sushmita Aunty kept jiggling.

"O God! This morning when the darkness disappears, may the sun of our lives rise and shine," I prayed to the Almighty.

The doctor's report finally came at 10 O'clock in the morning. Shruti was out of danger. Sushmita Aunty's tears finally stopped.

"She will be shifted from ICU to a private room in the evening. She needs your care and support for complete recovery. There is some damage which will take time to heal," the doctor remarked.

The news made us happy. The sun finally rose in our lives. In the evening, as the doctor had said, Shruti was transferred to a private room. The doctor had advised one

month's bed-rest for her. Two days later it would have been her birthday, the same day she was destined to depart for Jamshedpur, her hometown. How sad!

I was not the first to meet Shruti; in fact, I preferred Uncle and Aunty to go first. They needed to have some quality time with their daughter. Shruti was their only wealth and they had had the bitter experience of nearly losing it. After some time Uncle came out and said, "Go inside and meet her. She is very disturbed. She needs you," I entered the room. There was a peculiar smell of medicines in the room which turned me off. Shruti was lying on the bed. Both her legs were fractured and rested on the hanging sling. There were bandages on her head and hands. Cerebral haemorrhage had taken a toll on her. Dark circles around her eyes and tears on the cheeks made her look miserable. I touched her hand and said, "Hey! Don't worry. Everything will be fine."

She blinked her eyes. I kept caressing her hands. When you undergo such a disaster, you are hurt physically as well as mentally. Her body said of the physical pain and her eyes expressed the inner pain.

"You are going home. There, Uncle and Aunty will take care of you. You are going to be well very soon," I consoled. She nodded.

"I am happy to see you," her voice was too low. I smiled back.

Suddenly she started groaning. Something was troubling her. I could feel it from the numbness of her hands.

"Prateek died in the blast," she said and tears poured from her eyes.

"What?" I gaped at her. Her sobs became loud enough. I did not know what to say.

Prateek and Shruti were hanging out at CP when the bomb blast took place. His body was charred into pieces. Shruti was physically damaged, emotionally traumatised and mentally unbalanced. She had lost her love and the hope of her life. It was too much for her. Is this what those fucking fanatics enjoy doing for their religion? Spectators, perpetrators and sufferers! Out of these three, the last one is the worst. And we Indians are very good at being that. When I told Sushmita Aunty about Prateek, she was also in tears. She pretty well understood her daughter's emotions.

I came out of the room. I did not want to face Shruti any longer as she kept wincing with pain. Fate acted cruel to her. My consolation could not have done any miracle, so I walked out and sat in the lounge. The television in the corner caught my attention. The news anchor was dissecting the aftermath of blasts with some analysts. The marquee on the screen said, '*Over 50 killed and 100 injured in Delhi blasts.*'

I knew one from each category. Media keeps talking, the government keeps promising and people keep suffering.

That is Incredible India! In our country, television and terrorism rule. A symbiotic relationship! We Indians are fond of *tamasha*. The one-hour debate talked of many things; it showed poignant videos of the sufferers with commercials in between. Imagine listening to a sad song with feet-tapping music in between the lyrics. These media people know how to market adversity. I felt a storm inside my mind. There was indignation for the system—the system which was too weak to act.

I stayed in Delhi for two more days. I tried to tell a lot of funny things to Shruti to make her feel better. I succeeded, but only partially. The day she was leaving for Jamshedpur, I gifted a bouquet. I could not find a better birthday gift. At the airport, Vijay Uncle said to me, "Son, we are really obliged by your gesture. We are indebted to you for the support you gave us. Take care of yourself," Sushmita Aunty kissed my forehead. I was overwhelmed. I waved as they walked their way to the plane.

In the evening, I took my train to Kota. A man sat on my berth as the train left the platform. His typical hair-cut and brawny body signalled towards his military background.

"Hello! Are you from military?" I asked.

"Yeah," the man sitting on my berth replied.

"Do you mind if I continue sitting here? Actually I have a lot of luggage and my ticket is unconfirmed," he asked me.

He probably thought that I was uncomfortable with his presence.

"No, absolutely not," I spontaneously responded and continued, "it is because of you guys that I am still alive, otherwise those bastards would have killed me too." My emotions erupted like a volcano. Anger and fart, both need a vent, otherwise they can be harmful.

He looked at me with an enigmatic smile and then asked for an explanation at my abrupt remark. I narrated everything to him.

"I can understand your pain. There are thousands like you. It is really sad for mankind. Those lunatics have turned into cannibals. You know, we are competent enough to overpower them within twenty-four hours. But due to political and diplomatic reasons we are restrained," he said.

"But are those reasons bigger than innocent lives? Why should we tolerate it?"

Frustration was evident in my voice. He nodded and said, "Yes, you are right. Perhaps our country needs a revolution. And it is young people like you who can make a change," he patted my shoulder. His hands were really strong. He continued, "I have lost many friends in the Kargil war. It is hard to digest, but life goes on. So, be brave and move ahead."

"So, how many victims your gunshots made?" I asked.

"I don't remember but I killed many of them. But I did get hurt too," he smiled and showed the mark of a bullet on his left shoulder. I really felt proud of sharing my berth with that person. He was the real hero and there were many more like him. Had there been more guys like him, there would have been no terrorists and no blasts in our country. Before stepping down from the train at Kota, I shook hands with him. "You guys are the real heroes of India. We don't need a revolution but more people like you."

His eyes sparkled with tears.

* * *

"Thank God! She is allright. I really feel sorry for her. But you did not contact me once. I was missing you badly," Aditi was annoyed.

"I was too much involved with Shruti. She needed me. Anyway, I am sorry for that. I hope you understand." The fatigue of journey was still in my eyes. Dark circles had appeared around my eyes due to insufficient sleep.

"Yeah, it is okay," she smiled back.

"But the trouble does not end for me."

"What trouble?" she asked.

"I missed the test. Vivek told me that the authority is going to take strict action against poor performers and absentees," I replied.

"But you have a genuine reason."

"I know, but it would be hard to convince them."

She nodded and kissed, but suddenly stopped midway. "I am angry with you. You again broke your promise," she looked away from me.

"What promise?" I had no inkling.

"Cigarettes," her nose flared with anger. I had smoked heavily in the last two days. The last one I lit was half an hour ago. She must have smelt it.

"Oh! Sweetheart, I am really sorry. I promise I will not repeat it. It just happened. I was so tense and I..."

"No excuse. Take out your packet and hand it over to me," she interrupted.

I took out the cigarette packet.

"And lighter too."

"Okay, *Baba*," I gave it away as I had no other choice. Without any delay she threw it in a dustbin.

"What pleasure do you guys derive from smoking? Don't you understand that it is injurious to health?" she continued her bossy tone.

"Okay, Madam! I forgot that my girlfriend is a Hitler. I don't have a tail, otherwise I would have wagged that to pay my obeisance to you," sometimes you have to say nasty things to fawn a lady. She could not stop her laugh. Even though I had just suffered a loss of hundred bucks, I smiled

back. I should have kept a mouth-freshener with me. Anyway, next time! Learn from your mistakes and repeat them without getting caught.

The next day I had to meet Prof. Khanna. He was the administrative head of the Apex Institute and was well-known for his repulsive personality. I braced myself for the meet.

"How is his mood?" I asked a guy coming out of his office. He looked agitated.

"Terrible," he replied.

Prof. Khanna was sitting in an armchair boasting his paunch. The man was over 120 kilograms. He was entertaining someone who sat facing him.

"Good morning, sir. I am Abhi Sharma from Target course. I could not appear in the last test, so I was asked to report to you."

The other person sitting in the room turned his head around to see the intruder. I was surprised to see Prof. Sen. I was not expecting two devils.

"Why do you guys come to Kota for preparations? Sit at your home and watch movies. Have fun. There is no reason in wasting time here. Taking tests is a futile exercise. Eh?" Prof. Khanna looked at me with disdain.

Before I could say anything the second devil quipped. "How can he even think of appearing in an exam? Mr Sharma remains absent minded during lectures. He bunks classes. Earlier he had been suspended from my class. He is an absolute crap. Dung-cake!"

"No, sir. Actually, one of my close relatives died in the recent terrorist blast and another one was badly injured. I have been in Delhi for the last four days and came back only yesterday. I promise you that I will not miss any test in future," I said with conviction.

"Well, I am no fool to believe you. I run this place and know everything you guys do."

"Sir, believe me. I am telling the truth. Why would I sabotage my career?" I pleaded with Prof. Khanna.

"It is useless to talk to you guys. You will get the same punishment as everyone else is going to get. You will be demoted to a lower batch and a letter will be sent to your parents. Go to my assistant and complete the formalities," he directed.

There was no point in arguing with him. He was the boss and I, a slave to his whims.

"And before you go, I warn you, leave your devil-may-care attitude or you are going to spoil your future. Learn from your mistakes," Prof. Sen said with a sarcastic smile. His eyes were scornful. I was disheartened.

I went to Mr Khanna's assistant. Unlike his boss, he was chummy.

"Sir, we have met earlier. Do you remember Raju's tea-stall?" I tried to strike a soft corner. He was regular at the tea-stall. We had had a few conversations a couple of times.

"Yeah, I do," he said and took out a letter from a file. "Here is the letter. Sign it and keep a xerox copy with you. The original one will be sent to your parents."

"Can't you help somehow?" I looked at him with hope.

"No, if I do, I will lose my job. By the way, before you go, submit your identity card at the reception counter. From tomorrow you will have to attend classes in the last batch."

"What? Last batch? This is too much," I was exasperated. He gave an I-can't-help look.

"Please sir, you are close to Prof. Khanna. You know me. I am far from bad. Please advocate for my case," I requested.

"See, I understand your problem. I overheard you guys, but Mr Khanna is an obstinate man. For him rules are everything," he put his hand on my shoulder and continued, "Don't worry about the demotion. Keep attending lectures in the same batch. No one is going to ever find out which batch you belong to. But keep it off the record." The soft corner finally made its presence.

"Thanks a lot."

Tea-stalls, hair saloons and betel shops are the places where you get a chance to widen your social circle. And if you are tactful, you score. I scored twice, first with Raghu *bhaiya* and partially with Mr Khanna's assistant.

Next few days I cut down my meetings with Aditi. I devoted most of my time to studies. I was taking time for my feelings to sink in. My father got the letter. The language was so provocative that it could have made any father furious. But he knew the truth. He was proud of his son. Shruti was recovering well and everybody felt happy for her. As far as the lectures were concerned, I never attended any lecture in the last batch. New Year was coming and I was waiting eagerly for it.

Joker's Jottings

If I ever come across a terrorist, do you know what I am gonna do before shooting him in head? Pee on him, fill his mouth with dog's crap and then castrate him. Hideous bastards!

And Mr Khanna, a fat rodent who needs to be kept in a zoo was a biological weapon. His paunch aka fart-pot stunk. Air, please.

Chapter Nine

Ranthambore, Pill & Bakra

"Ranthambore," Naidu suggested.

The name was familiar to me. I had read about it in my social studies book. "That wildlife sanctuary!" I exclaimed.

"Yes, Bro. It is a wonderful place. Situated in Sawai Madhopur, it is around 100 kilometers away from here," Naidu explained.

"Do we stay there at night?" Rohan asked.

"Only if they don't bring their girls with them," Naidu said, pointing towards me and Vivek.

"C'mon guys. Do you expect me and Riya not to stay together on New Year's Day? We can start early so that we have plenty of time," Vivek said.

I gave mute support.

"Okay. So the plan is final. We will be leaving for Ranthambore on 1st January at 6 a.m. sharp in the morning," Rohan announced.

"What about the money?" I asked.

"Well, it is a thousand bucks each, but you two are going to pay for girls too," Naidu replied.

Having a girlfriend is not always pleasant. It always comes at an exorbitant price.

"And what do we do tomorrow night?' Vivek asked.

"Let us salute the passing year with dance and drinks," I said.

"Yippee!" everybody screamed.

Drinking makes you a better dancer. I was always counted among the best dancers my school ever produced. Besides, it was my USP among girls. Dance is always a turn-on for girls. 31st December night, we drank. We danced and we bumbled on the roads. We were frenzied and a thrill of craziness kept pumping adrenalin in our veins. At 2 a.m. we decided to take a nap so that we remained fresh for the Ranthambore trip.

We left Kota by car at 7 a.m. The interior of the car was spacious enough to make all of us comfortable.

"Aditi! Do you know, Abhi is an awesome dancer? Last

night he electrified our *adda* with his rocking moves," Naidu said.

Aditi gave me a you-never-told-me look.

"Thanks for the compliment. Actually I learnt to dance at a music academy in Jamshedpur. I was always a star performer. My dance teacher even egged me on to take dance as a career," I disclosed my dexterity.

Aditi smiled. She too was fond of dancing. She always told me how eager she was to learn belly dancing. Belly dancing! Shakira does it. Yummy!

"So, have you guys made any resolution?" Riya asked the same clichéd question. She was sitting with Vivek on the back seat.

"Yes, I have resolved to study for more than 12 hours a day and avoid cyber cafes completely," Naidu confessed. Except Riya and Aditi, we all laughed.

"What an absurd joke, Naidu!" I remarked and continued, "we all know that you cannot even follow it for a week."

"I have decided to love Riya more than ever," Vivek said, while fondling Riya's hair. "We stay inseparable." Love was in the air for them.

"Oh! Come on. Don't start your love *raga* here. Keep it for next time," Naidu said. He turned towards Rohan and then resumed. "Don't you think that we are party poopers on their honeymoon?" Aditi and Riya gave a shy smile.

"There is no problem. Naidu and Rohan make a great pair. I assume we are three couples," Vivek laughed loudly at Naidu. Naidu gave a mocking smile.

"Why don't we play something?" I suggested.

"Dumb charades." Aditi quipped.

Playing dumb charades is always fun especially when your opponents act weirdo on the pretext of nasty names you give to them. Rohan, Aditi and I were on the same side. The game continued till we reached our destination at 9:55 a.m. We won 4-2.

Ranthambore, a wildlife sanctuary, is known for tigers that have become scarce in India. Spread over hundreds of acres, it is a hotspot among tourists. There was a *mela* of foreign tourists. For them, India still happens to be the land of snakes and tigers.

"Dude, see her. Is not her dress too provoking?" Naidu pointed towards a foreign tourist who was in shorts and her top was far from being opaque. I nodded. The only benefit of foreign tourists coming to India is that we get a chance to have some quality NSP.

"Now you tell me, why does she wear such a dress if it can arouse hormones in some rowdies? Anyone can offend her."

"Are you aroused?" I nudged Naidu.

"Honestly yes, but I can control my testosterone."

"Well, she is too fair for you. Don't even think of that," I retorted.

"Here are the tickets. Our safari starts in ten minutes," Vivek returned from the ticket counter.

"Is not this place very appealing?" Aditi said as we moved towards the entry point.

"Yeah," I responded.

"I have never been to any sanctuary. You know, my mother loves animals. We have a pet at our home. I really miss him," she was in a cheery mood and excited about the safari.

"Good morning to all of you. My name is Vikram Singh and I am your guide for this trip." A man in blue uniform interrupted our conversation. He grinned and resumed, "Next few hours you are going to enjoy the beauty and thrill of the jungle. But beware and take care of yourself and your friends. There are offshoots of trees hanging over the path. So keep your heads low and safe," he gave a stupid smile.

In the next half an hour our jeep penetrated deep into the jungle. We came across several species of animals and trees. The guide spilled out their names but most of them were tongue-twisters. The jeep stopped in front of a monstrous tree.

"All of you step down. This is an area where you can roam freely. You will find deer, stags and beautiful birds.

They are harmless and absolutely delightful to watch. We start again in half an hour," Vikram Singh announced.

"And please do not litter the area," he appealed to all the visitors.

The roads were nothing less than a maze.

"Let us go to some calm place. It is too crowded," I said to Aditi.

She held my hand and we took a byroad.

"Sweetheart, being with you gives me a sense of completeness. I feel ecstatic with you." My hands encircled her cheeks. We chose to sit beneath an old tree. There were no noises. Everybody was too far and we were insulated from them.

"Abhi! You are the most wonderful thing that has happened to me."

I looked in her eyes. They said, 'take me in your arms'. We huddled to make ourselves cozy. The sound of leaves rustling in the breeze played the music. Whirling leaves danced their way down to fall on us. It was the tree's style of saying— 'Welcome'.

"Why were you looking wistfully at that foreign bitch?" Aditi complained.

"No, I was not," I faked innocence.

"Don't lie. I saw you staring at her."

"But my intentions were not bad," I tried to justify.

"Am I a fool?"

"Why are you over-reacting? I know, you feel jealous. Isn't it?"

She kept silent and continued caressing my ears. I pinched her shoulder and dropped my hands down to her breasts.

"This is my Everest," I remarked.

"Everests," she rectified me.

"These are now my assets," I smiled. My right hand entered inside her top. I touched the evcrests. I pressed them really hard. Every time I tried to close my hands, she gave an expression of silent moan. The pleasure kept us going. She unbuttoned my shirt. I lay down on the ground and her peaks rested on my chest. The air was getting sultry and hotter. Her tongue moved into my mouth. Vigorously and wildly! Our first smooch was gentle and nervous but the numerous practices we made in movie halls had made us experts. We unleashed our passions. Her hands groped for something below my navel. I unbuckled my belt and she unzipped my jeans.

"I like the sound of unzipping," she said.

I glued my lips to brownish peaks. It was already taut. Her left hand crawled over my snake.

"It is too gigantic and the balls are too cute to fondle," she brazenly remarked. With every small movement of her fingers I felt a raunchy sensation in my organ. The temperature and testosterone level shot high in the sky. Suddenly my obnoxious phone made its presence marked.

"Hello! Where are you two guys? We all are waiting for you. Come soon," Vivek on the other side commanded.

"Okay. In two minutes," I said.

Reluctantly we dressed ourselves and hurried to catch the group. On our way we held hands tightly. The passionate moments made us yearn for more intimacy. We enjoyed the incomplete romance completely.

"Where were you?" Naidu asked. All eyes were staring at us.

"Actually, we lost the way. Sorry for the inconvenience caused to you guys," I apologised.

"You got something in your hair," Vivek said. He looked tense. He lent a hand and ruffled my hand. Some hay and twigs fell down. I looked at Aditi. She winked and smiled. We both were responsible for those twigs.

Our safari ended at 3:00 p.m. It was exciting and tiresome. We could not spot any tigers. Either they were scarce or they were on a vacation. Either way, it was human fault.

"I am starving. Let us have some food," I said. We walked to a nearby *dhaba*.

"I never thought that you could be so wild," I whispered

in Aditi's ears. She tweaked me on thighs and said, "Don't worry. The best is yet to come." Those words resonated in my mind. It is so beautiful to hear from a girl.

"Abhi! Come with me for a second," Vivek signalled to me. He took me near our car.

"What is the matter? Why are you being so secretive?" I asked.

"Well, how do I say?"

"C'mon yaar, tell me."

"Riya and I had sex."

"What! Are you a nerd? Why did you do the *chutiyaap*?" I looked at him with astonishment. Humans are no less than animals when left free. In fact, they are even more dangerous than animals. And amongst the two of us, he had gone wilder to shatter all the barriers.

"I know it was crazy to do so, but it was impulsive. Now I don't know what to do? Can you think of a way out?" he was desperate.

"I still don't understand why the hell you chose a wildlife sanctuary to have sex with your girlfriend? It is irrational. Anyway, give me some time to find out alternatives."

Vivek and Riya made their honeymoon right there in the sanctuary's daylight. Unfortunately, Riya's menstrual cycle was over a week back and Vivek did not use any protection. The possibility of an unwanted pregnancy loomed over her.

Somewhere in my mind I felt happy that Aditi and I were stopped midway, otherwise I would have also opened the Pandora's box.

"What do we do?" I kept muttering and jiggled. However strong and tough you are, there are some situations in life where you feel helpless and hopeless. Vivek was going through the same phase. His face exuded despair.

"See, first of all, keep it a secret. The less number of people know the better it is for you," I suggested. "And don't worry, I will not tell Aditi about this," I assured him. He still looked agitated.

"For now, cheer up. We will fix it. Let's think over it," I consoled.

Our return journey started at 4:00 p.m. Sex had always been an area of interest for me. I belonged to the generation of World Wide Web where porn is ubiquitous. Searching, reading, watching and enjoying are practiced by millions of netizens. I was no exception. In the process I had developed a high sex quotient. I knew about orgasms, g-spot, contraceptives and sundry things more than my peers.

'Copper-T....abortion in a clinic....oral pills....what?.... But copper-T is for prevention....going to a clinic is too dangerous....if the news leaks, it will be a disaster.' Thoughts smothered me. I tried to explore every avenue of opportunity. All the time, while on the return journey, Vivek and Riya looked gloomy. Every passing moment was dialling anxiety in them. Poor guys, their amorous experience was giving them a tough time.

We dropped Aditi and Riya at their hostel at 7:30 p.m.

"Tonight, stay at my place," I said to Vivek. He had no other choice. He knew I was the only one who could help him.

We bade goodbye to Naidu and Rohan and walked towards Jaiswal villa.

"Let me buy some cigarettes," Vivek said.

Cigarettes taste best when you are unhappy. They are quintessential of the human sadness and anxiety.

"Did you find some way?" Vivek asked.

"I am a bit confused. Besides, how can you be so sure that she is going to get pregnant? Maybe fertilisation did not take place," I suggested.

"No, Bro. I cannot take a chance. I have already made a mistake and if I don't rectify it, we are screwed. Maybe we can go to some clinic."

"Not at all. You cannot go for abortion at such an early stage. Besides, a girl's chastity remains at risk in such a step. You cannot trust anyone. We need to find a way out so that Riya's identity remains undisclosed."

I myself did not know how to deal with teenage pregnancy but I talked like an expert. Self-confidence! All thanks to internet.

"Do you know someone who has been in such a situation or who can help us?" he asked

His question was inspired from Raghu *bhaiya* episode.

"No," I said.

We kept our grey cells at work.

"Wait.......I know someone," I pierced the minute-long silence.

"Who?" Vivek was too impatient.

"Aman, my elder brother. He is a doctor. He must be knowing some way out of this," I said.

Without giving a second thought, I called my brother. He was six years older to me. A brilliant student since childhood, he was a great doctor in making. He was doing his further studies along with practice. We really had spent a lot of quality time together. After his standard XII exams, he got admission in AIIMS. Since then our closeness suffered. The older you grow the distant you get from your siblings.

"Hi, *bhaiya*! How are you?" I asked

It took me five minutes to narrate him the whole story. Before I hung up I requested *bhaiya* to keep everything a secret.

"Don't worry, *Chhotu*. Take care of yourself," he assured me. He always called me 'Chhotu'. I loved the name. It gave a sense of affection and security.

"What did he say?" Vivek looked curiously at me.

I looked at him broodily. It made him more nervous.

"Unwanted-100," I grinned.

"What is that?"

"Give her one tablet within 72 hours and all your fucking sperms will turn impotent. No chance of pregnancy," I explained.

My words electrified him. He hugged me and lifted me in air.

"Aman *bhaiya* rocks," he yelled.

"Well, hold on. There is a small problem. We need a doctor's prescription to get this medicine."

"What?" His smile vanished like a dwindling flame.

"See your face," I laughed.

"Why are you laughing?" he asked.

"I was just joking. We don't need any prescription. This medicine is much like a condom, available to all. It is new, so people do not know about it."

"You bastard!" he punched me hard in the stomach. I leaned away.

"Let us go to the chemist shop," he said.

"Now?"

"Yes, Bro! The sooner I fix this the better for me."

At 10 p.m. we went to Riya's hostel. Unfortunately, the warden happened to be present there. I had seen her a couple of times before. The lady was a frustrated, fat Hitler. She was as repulsive as a pig.

"What are you two doing here?" the bespectacled lady fired the question at us.

"Good evening, Madam. We are friends of Riya. Actually she was not feeling well, so she asked me to bring some medicines for her," I was unruffled unlike Vivek.

"Okay. Give it to me. I will give it to her," she sounded harsh. Every girl's hostel warden suffers from a prejudice for guys. Vivek handed the pill to her. She took it on her palm and started examining it. Now this was fatal for us. What if she knows about the pill? I got jitters at the thought. Vivek nudged me.

"These are anti-allergic," I tried to stop her from further examination.

"Okay. You two can go," she gave us a look as if we were beggars outside her palace. Bloody pig!

Five minutes later, Vivek called up Riya and explained everything to her.

"Happy now?" I asked.

"Yes. I feel relieved."

"So the lady Hitler did not create any troubles."

He nodded. The warden herself delivered the contraceptive pill to Riya. Ignorance is bliss!

"Now let us sleep. I am really tired. The first day of the year was really whacky," I sounded exhausted.

"I have brought this for you," Vivek took out something from his pocket and put on my palm. Utterly insane. He gifted me two condoms. I gave him a startled look.

"But why?"

"I made a mistake. Now I will always keep it with me. You also do the same. I saw twigs and leaves in your hair. I too got them," he alluded. I smiled. I understood his allusions.

"A narrow escape!" I remarked.

We never told anyone about the incident. Some things are better when kept cagey.

"JEE, AIEEE, DCE, VIT, CUSAT and Karnataka CET. I am going for all of them," Vivek said.

"Why not the other state engineering colleges? Why six? Make it a score of at least twelve," I taunted.

"You know there are lakhs of aspirants fighting for a few thousand seats. More exams I appear, better are the chances of my admission," he backfired at me.

"Yes, I second that. I have also applied for seven places. If I don't make into an engineering college, all my relatives are going to snigger at me," Naidu too supported Vivek.

"I am going for just three—JEE, BITS and AIEEE. What about you Rohan?" I asked.

We all knew that Rohan's chance of making it big was highest amongst us.

"IIT-JEE and AIEEE only. It is better not to waste

money and time on second-tier institutes. There is a quality crunch and in addition to that, their placements are below average," he was confident.

"But everyone is not as bright as you. What about the average people?" Naidu questioned Rohan's ideology.

"That does not mean that you will compromise with quality. We all want to be technocrats. Here, quality matters. We all are born in a generation which is money-minded and hysteric about management, medical and engineering. IITs are reputed for their quality and technical know-how. It is overcrowding in this field that has led to mushrooming of private colleges all across the country. They loot and deceive you by giving a fucking degree." Nuggets of wisdom were flowing from his mouth. His hands moved more than his lips. We listened carefully to his crap discourse. Seeing his listeners gave him confidence to continue. "In fact the coaching industry is also a by-product of this make-me-engineer phenomenon. We are paying lakhs of rupees here and they give us negligence, frustration and depression in return."

"Come on. Cut your crap. Be practical. We are not desperate for a degree from a top college. In the end, most of us want to do management. All we need is an MBA degree from some IIM," Vivek interrupted him.

"Rohan! What you are saying is true. We all belong to

this academic-hysteric generation but all we aim for is a plush salary and a plethora of perquisites. Come June and I hope that each one of us gets to a good place," I too tried to churn out wise words.

"Well said, dude! We want to have what makes us happy. You would be astonished to know that last year one of my friends paid ten lakhs to buy a seat in a little known engineering college in Maharashtra. Besides, the annual fee is above two lakhs," Naidu said.

"This is nothing. I know a boy who used impersonation to crack an entrance exam. Those silly invigilators could not even figure it out," Vivek proclaimed.

"This business is too rampant these days. All the insiders know about it. Anyway, everything is fair in love and war. Everything sells," Rohan said.

On hearing the word 'love,' Aditi came to my mind. Last night we had had a small fight. Silly issues, sillier fights and loads of tears are an integral part of romance. She was too stubborn to say a 'sorry'. So I typed a SMS to her.

'Sorry sweetheart, cud not sleep whole nite. Pillow wet with tears. Can't live a moment widout u; missing u badly.' Everything was a lie except the last part. But isn't an exaggeration fair in love?

"I have heard that around thirty thousand students are appearing for the test scheduled on 15th January." The discussion continued with Naidu's disclosure.

"The numbers are going to increase with every test. This time I will leave no stones unturned. I have to perform this time," Vivek said with conviction. We all nodded in agreement.

A beep distracted me. Aditi's reply arrived.

'Same here. I 2 felt bad. Busy wid assignments. Meet u 2morow. Luv u. muah.'

I felt happy.

Next day I got an unknown call in the noon.

"Hello! Is this Mr Abhi Sharma?" a female voice said.

"Yes, may I know who this is?" I asked.

"Good afternoon, Mr Sharma. I am Vaishali Wadhwani from V-first. I am glad to inform that you have won a bounty of fifty thousands in our sweepstakes. Congratulations for that."

"Oh! Thanks a lot. But I didn't get you."

"I'll explain. First, I would like to confirm your number and e-mail address. Your mobile number is 9929997378 and e-mail id is abhi.sharma@gmail.com."

"Yes," I said.

"Well Mr Sharma, you have won an i-pod, a Timex wrist watch worth ten thousand, lifetime membership of our book club, a goodie bag and books worth four thousand."

"That's great!" I exclaimed.

"Absolutely. We will deliver all these items at your doorstep within a week, but you will have to pay a token amount of three thousand. This is a part of company's policy and besides it was also mentioned in the conditions of sweepstakes," Vaishali said.

"But."

"Don't worry for anything. The whole process is quite easy and transparent. May I have your credit card details?"

"I don't have one. All I have is a debit card," I said.

"No problem. You can make online payment through it. Once you do it, we will dispatch the stuff to your address."

"Madam, I think I need some time to think over it," I said patiently.

"Okay, take your own time. I have mailed you the details. Do check it and I will get back to you tomorrow. Have a nice day!" she hung up.

V-first was a small company, mainly into online shopping business. A few days back when I was surfing the net, I came across its site where I registered for sweepstakes. What's bad in filling a form if it shows you the way to a treasure? I finally hit the jackpot. The New Year seemed to be announcing good times ahead.

Had I told my mother about it, I would have received serious rebuke from her. Rohan was the wisest friend I had, so I thought of seeking his advice.

"Can you trust them?" Rohan asked.

"I don't know but it is too tempting," I said.

"There is a strong possibility that everything is a trap. You may become a victim of online phishing," he warned.

The whole world has witnessed rapid scientific and economic development, but there is no denying that the scene regrading trust has worsened. Irrespective of fields, nowadays trust is scarce! Count the number of people you trust and you will end before you start.

"Aditi's birthday is on the 20th of January. I had kept aside a few thousand rupees for the gift. I think if I get an I-pod, then it would be the most memorable gift for her," I said.

Aditi loved music. An I-pod would be the most apt thing for her birthday. In addition to that, giving an expensive gift to your girlfriend makes you feel rich and proud, even though the reality may be opposite.

"Well, if that is the case, then it is apposite. Go ahead with it," Rohan approved.

In fact I had already taken that decision; all I wanted was somebody's support. I paid three thousand bucks to V-first. Every time I imagined giving the gift to Aditi, I felt like giving the Taj Mahal to her.

'*Wow! You bought this for me. I love you, my sugarplum. It is so lovely.*' Those imaginary words of her echoed in my mind. Next whole week, preparations for the coming test and the

anxious wait for the courier from V-first kept me preoccupied. I tried to call up Vaishali Wadhwani a few times, but the incoming facility on her number was debarred. I also made a few mail queries, all of which were replied back asking me to keep patience. Patience, it sucks.

On 12th January, a courier arrived. It was from V-first. I was very glad to see it. I unwrapped the packet wildly to find some books, some documents, a goodies bag but no wrist watch or i-pod. The immense joy that I gathered on seeing the packet faded away. A letter addressed to me said:

Dear Mr Abhi Sharma

V-first is glad to induct you in its book club. We are sending you lifetime membership card enclosed with this letter. Please do find your goodies bag and a set of books with this letter. As a part of our company's policy, every member of the book club has to deposit a sum of one thousand annually. At the end of first year, we will send a wrist-watch and as soon as you complete two years of membership, you will receive an i-pod......

I did not read further. It made no sense. All my expectations were razed. The evanescence of my joy was melancholic. I have seen people being victimised on shows like, MTV Bakra. In real life Vaishali Wadhwani and her company made me a *bakra*. I kept muttering swearwords for that bitch Vaishali. I felt pissed off. I kept the set of books on my table. Interestingly, one of the books said. '*Greed: Nemesis of Mankind.*' How true! I thought.

Joker's Jottings

In a male body the devil resides at three places; mind, heart and fleshy snake protruding down the waist. The first two are at times docile, but the last one is always formidable. Vivek unbridled it in the middle of a sanctuary without the snake's mask. Phodu*!*

Well what's your awareness on sex barometer? Ask your teacher to conduct a GD on condom, pills and more. Let knowledge spread.

Chapter Ten

Chor & Police

"You can go to the consumer forum. Report the case to them," Vivek suggested.

"No guys. Take the bird's view. There is no legal loophole in their fraud. Besides they have promised to give everything in future. Everything is impeccable," Rohan dissected the scenario for us.

"Huh! My legs are very eager to kick that whore's ass," anger was still simmering inside me.

"Who? Vaishali Wadhwani?" Vivek gave a wide grin. I nodded. I was too desperate and restless to retaliate.

"I bent to pluck the rose and all I got are thorns all over

the face and horns on the head," I said with disgust on my face.

"Waah, Waah," everyone in the room clapped and shouted.

"What a beautiful description!" Naidu remarked and started a new tune *"Teri gaand me danda, teri gaand me danda reeeeee.....ye kya Vaishali ne kar dala re...... Oooo.....tera chutiya kaat daala reeeee.....ye kya Vaishali ne kar dala re...."*

"Stop it, you motherfucker. Come on guys. Don't make me feel poor," I said and continued, "what happened with me is a classic example of unethical marketing. When you place profit above ethics, you automatically get perverted. All tactics! This is what they teach in management—how to build trust on a heap of lies and then burn a hole in your pockets. All in a sophisticated way! White-collared dacoits. Someday I would be also doing the same."

They all nodded. Marketing and entrepreneurship always held my interest. One reason for this was my father and the other one was that I wanted to rake in moolah, early and easily. Alas, I experienced the grey side of it! The timing was completely inappropriate.

How do I manage a gift for Aditi? And even if I do, then how do I make up for the monetary loss? I kept nagging myself. Problems always come in pairs.

"Don't brood over this. Whatever happened, let us forget it. Now focus on the day after tomorrow's test," Rohan

patted my shoulder. It did not make me feel better but at least he tried for it. I gave a dejected nod.

The comprehensive syllabus for the test exacerbated the scene for me. I turned a few pages of the *Concepts of Physics*. The book is omnipresent; the author is omniscient, only the readers are not omnipotent enough to solve the sums. While some students worshipped HCV's COP, others, like me, made it an object of blasphemy.

"HCV's COP is the *Gita*, *Quran*, *Bible*, *Guru Granth Sahib*, depending upon the religion you belong to. Read it religiously." one of the teachers at Apex Institute remarked.

Quite true! All are hard to digest. To celebrate my struggle with sums, I started scribbling on my notebook.

'Mechanics suck, mechanics suck.'

I kept it doing for a while till my phone rang. "Hi Shruti! How are you?" I said.

"Thank God. You still recognise my voice. I thought you forgot me. Anyway I am fine. How about you?"

I had promised her to call up daily but I did not do so even once in the last few days.

"No, *Yaar*. I have an exam day after tomorrow. So was quite busy in preparations; lost under immense pressure! Anyway, how is your recovery now?"

"Gave away crutches! Now I walk freely. I will go back to Delhi by the end of this month," her voice was cheery.

"Oh! That is great."

"Only the scars are left."

Few seconds earlier her voice was joyous and suddenly the tone fell down. She started sobbing. It was the Prateek factor.

"Hey! Stop crying. Prateek loved you a lot and he would always stay in your heart. Be brave and take care yourself. That is the call of the hour."

The best way to forget pain is to divert attention. Pain starts in the brain and ends there only.

"Yeah, I know. I have to move on. All these have changed me a lot. Anyway, you carry on your work. All the best for your exam."

"Goodnight! Sweet dreams."

"Goodnight," she hung up.

'Poor girl!' I thought.

"I don't believe that you fared so well. You were not even half prepared for that!" Aditi exclaimed.

"Every one of us has an infinite hidden potential. You never know when it comes out."

"Don't boast so much. The paper was relatively easy and you could not even answer a single question of rotational mechanics correctly," she taunted me.

"Well, there is a reason for that. You must not forget that I was not allowed to attend classes of rotational mechanics as

I was under suspension. And for your kind information, all my friends found the paper to be tough. I have fared much better than all of them," I retorted.

"Then I have a reason to ask for a treat," she gave a grin. We walked towards a *chaat* stall. Every time the pocket didn't allow to eat kingsize. After all I had to manage money for her gift also.

"By the way, next week we are having revision classes of rotation. Why don't you attend them?" she suggested.

"How can I attend classes in your institute?"

"Nowadays, they don't check identity cards. So it is simple to walk inside the class. And our physics teacher is the icing on the cake. Prof. KK! You must have heard."

Prof. KK was a gem. Amongst students he was nick-named as God of mechanics. Earlier he was a faculty member of Apex Institute but two years back, he migrated to Toppers' Institute. There were many stories explaining his migration. Some said that it was a money factor while others said his rising popularity and internal politics of faculty members were to blame.

"Okay, Madam, I will see it. You first eat this," I handed a cheese burger to her.

My phone beeped. It was an SMS from Naidu.

'Come 2 my room by 9. We r going 2 chor bazaar tonight. Keep cash with u."

I looked at the watch. It was 6:45 p.m. More than hundred hours were still remaining for Aditi's birthday. 20th January was a much awaited day for me. It was the first birthday of my first love with me. I was in a mood to make it a red-lettered day in the life of Aditi. Super special! Aditi bade me goodbye with a kiss. It was not a big deal for us. We now knew better places where we had no company. A walk across those lanes and we relished kissing and touching.

"Welcome Mr *Phodu*," Vivek started the refrain and Naidu joined him. The sound of *Phodu* coupled with claps echoed in the room. It continued for almost a minute till I interrupted, "Now please stop the crap."

"Whoo-hoo! See the *Phodu's* smile."

Phodu was the hindi equivalent of 'geek'. The reason for the titular honour was my unexpected performance in the last test. Everybody counted me as a bad performer!

"We never knew that we had a hidden genius amongst us," Vivek's leg-pulling continued.

"Come on, guys. You also know that my preparations were insufficient for such a performance. Everything that happened in fluke. Still it feels great," I gave a boasting smile and continued,"if you people have any doubts, feel free to take my help. After all a friend in need is a friend indeed."

"Thanks for your kind gesture, you evergreen asshole! We have a lot of problems in mechanics. So when do we start,

Mr *Phodu*?" Vivek said and burst into laughter. The king inside my head was dethroned. He was familiar with my dexterity in mechanics.

"Anyway let us come to the business. When do we start for the Chor Bazaar?" I changed the course of discussion.

"It starts at 2 a.m. and continues till 6 in the morning. The place is 30 minutes away from here. We depart at 1," Naidu informed about the plan.

"Are you coming?" I asked Vivek.

"No."

It meant Naidu and I were only to go. Rohan was a bit depressed with his test performance. Yet he did not lose the temperament and preferred to study harder at his place. He never got what he deserved. Hard luck!

"I believe that none of us has ever been to a place like that."

Everyone looked at each other blankly. The assumption was right. So none of us had any idea about the modus operandi of the market! It meant things were going to be tough for me and Naidu. Anyway life is all about learning every day.

"Have you thought about what to buy?" Vivek asked.

"Well not exactly but I have some things on my mind."

"Like?"

"Like a digital camera or some gadget she would find useful."

"Love is really a deadly disease," he quipped.

"Still it is healthier to be ill," I remarked.

"You two carry on your crap. I am going to have a quick nap. This pain is really unbearable," Naidu reclined with his hands over his private parts.

"What happened?" I asked.

"Poor asshole!" Vivek laughed

I looked at him, demanding an explanation.

"Last night the man saw porn for hours. Since then he has jerked off half a dozen times. Consequently he is suffering from excruciating pain."

I could not control my laugh.

"Don't smile like a demon," Naidu said. He winced with pain. For a guy that is the worst kind of pain.

"He has been playing with hands since he was in tenth class and whenever he does it more than twice, he starts getting pain."

"Is it true?" I asked.

Naidu nodded.

We got the matter to feed our brains and next few hours went in discussing and analysing the boys' hand game. In a startling revelation, Vivek told me that he often used Vaseline and other creams. I did not bother to ask how and why.

We reached Mahal Bagh at 1:45 a.m. Tens of people were already roaming here and there.

"What are they doing here?" I pointed towards some of the women standing near the pavements.

"Whores!"

"What! You brought me to the prostitutes' ghetto!"

"Calm down, Bro! Mahal Bagh is the area of the city where all illegal activities happen. Don't worry, we will do our work and return as quickly as possible."

I had never been put in such a situation. The fear of unknown made me nervous. In Chor Bazaar the shops were pretty much like the normal roadside stalls. The only difference was in the nature of the goods sold. We accosted a stall owner.

"Bhai Saab! Do you sell digital cameras?" I asked.

"Which one you want—Chinese or branded?"

"Branded."

"I have only two brands—Sony and Panasonic," he took out two pieces and showed to us.

"Show those with above 7.0 mega pixels."

He handed me one of Panasonic.

"I have only one in the high category," he remarked.

I looked at the camera carefully.

"Is it original?" I whispered to Naidu.

"I think so," he skimmed it and replied back.

"Sir, this camera is very good. The quality, durability and its features are awesome."

"How much?" I interrupted the seller's marketing leverage.

"9,000."

"What?"

"Sir, the original one comes for 15,000 rupees."

"No, you are demanding excess. Neither are you giving any warranty nor any accessory that comes with it," I braced myself for the bargaining. These days only fools do buying without bargaining.

"Lower your price. We are regulars here. Besides, he is the son of Jaipur's Police Commissioner," Naidu said in an aggressive tone.

"Okay, you give 6000."

"No."

"We would not give a single penny more than 3,000," I added to Naidu's strong refusal.

"Sir, you are saying too less. How will I earn if I sell at so low price?" he pleaded.

"Look, last week my friend bought the same item for 2,500. I am paying you more than that. You yourself think, otherwise we have other places to go," I made a little movement to signal him that I might leave without a delay.

"Every week I have to give 500 rupees to those policemen," he pointed to a nearby police patrol party and continued, "And you still say that I am demanding too much. Okay, I can lower to 3,200 but that is final."

"Okay," we said in unison.

The deal was closed at 3,200 bucks. As a precautionary measure, we did not bring our cell phones and ATM cards. I took out four 1,000 notes and handed to the stall-owner. He was not more than 25 in age. His typical attire revealed his religious background.

"What's your name?" I asked in a token gesture.

"Azhar."

All of a sudden the sound of a bullet echoed in my ears. I turned back to see the source of the sound. What I saw was petrifying. Two men were firing on the police jeep. Simultaneously they were running away. Half dozen a gun shots already attacked the policemen. Everything was happening at the intersection, hardly 50 metres away from where we were standing. The whole thing created panic in the market. The police who were caught with their pants down geared up and started backfiring. A lot of people ran here and there. I looked at Naidu. His eyes were terrified.

"Run," I shrieked.

We took a by-road to the right of the stall where we were standing. As we ran, we heard a few cries. With every gun-shot, the hullabaloo amplified. Few seconds of running away and the sounds faded away. We kept running till we reached an auto-rickshaw. We panted heavily as we sat in the auto-rickshaw. Our bodies were covered with sweat. It is unusual to sweat on a January night. Our brains almost got numb.

For the rest of the night we kept silent. Although we had brought the camera with us but I forgot to take the change from Azhar. But who thinks of money in such a situation? Buying a gift for Aditi gave me a bitter experience, second time in a row. I never had witnessed such an incident in my life.

One day later, I was aghast to see the newspaper. The headline in the local section said: "*Raghvendra Verma killed in late night encounter at Mahal Bagh.*"

Below was the photo of Raghu *bhaiya*. I did not read further. I could not figure out the how and why of this development. I was there when all this was happening. Raghu *bhaiya* was not that evil.

"Happy birthday, sweetheart!"

"Thank you."

"Did you get the gift?"

"No."

"Okay, where are you right now?"

"Balcony."

"Go to your room and something is waiting for you beneath the pillow."

Girls love surprises and boys work hard to make it possible. The reverse is rare.

"Wow! It is lovely. Hold for a second. I want to read the card."

Riya was the one who planted the surprise under Aditi's pillow. In every love story, there are several characters like Riya and Naidu who make the story more loveable with their incalculable contributions.

"It is so beautifully written. I loved it. And thanks for the camera. I wish you were with me so that I could have taken a snap of us together," Aditi said in an elated tone.

"This was your first birthday with me and I wanted you to feel like the princess of the city. So..," I paused.

"So what?" she got curious.

"So I am sending you a few roses. Ram *bhaiya* is on his way to your room."

"What? Where are you right now?"

"Guess."

"At my hostel gate."

"Yes, baby."

"Wait, I am coming to the terrace."

Standing outside a girls' hostel at 12:10 at night is not a pleasant thing to do but I was driven by a passion to impress Aditi with blandishments.

"I spotted you," she screamed on the phone. I looked at the terrace and she was standing at the corner, waving roses at me.

"I love you."

"Me too."

I gave a flying kiss to her.

"Hey you!" A male sound came into my ears. It was crass. I was standing at the gate of the hostel. As I turned back, I saw two policemen on the other side of the road. Both were riding horses. Surprised, shocked and scared.

"Come here," one of them signalled to me.

"Yesss....sir," I stammered.

"What the hell are you doing here?"

"Nothing sir," I was afraid to speak. What do I do? I thought.

"Straying outside a girls' hostel at midnight?"

"No..no..no sir."

One of the policemen climbed down from the horse.

"What is your name?" he asked

"Abhi Sharma."

"Localite?"

"No, sir. I am from Jamshedpur."

"O! You are from Bihar."

"No, sir. Jharkhand," I rectified.

Our country is far behind in terms of general awareness. Even the literates do not keep the updates of the latest happenings. Jharkhand had separated from Bihar in 2000 but many people still don't know about it. Incredible India! Truly!

"So you are coming with us," he put his hands on my shoulders.

I wanted to ask 'where', but out of fear I could not do so.

"Sir, believe me, I was not doing anything wrong. The truth is that today is my girlfriend's birthday and I was here to give her roses."

"Good liar! Now let us go to the police station."

"Sir, please," I pleaded but to no use.

Surprising others often ends in shocking yourself. I was at the receiving end of the shock. I had never been on a horse before. Usually people ride it on their marriage day. But I was going to the police station—a feat not achieved by my contemporaries. I was really invaded by apprehensions.

"Agrawal Babu. Who is the guest with you?" the sentry at the Bada Nagar police station asked one of the policemen accompanying me.

"This kid was creating nuisance outside the girls' hostel," he smiled back at the sentry.

The sentry gave me a dirty look as if I had eve-teased his daughter. In India, people enjoy vilifying. It makes them feel superior. I was ordered to sit on a bench. After 10 minutes the S.H.O called me.

"What's your name?" he asked in a typical police baritone. The man was in his early forties.

"Abhi Sharma," I replied.

"So Mr Sharma, do you know that your wrongdoing can put you behind the bars? How can be people like you be so uncivilised?" he looked disappointed and angry.

"Sir, today is my girlfriend's birthday. So I went there to wish her," tears started pouring from my eyes. I was not brave enough to spend a single night behind the bars.

"You are a student. You should be bothered about your career. Why don't you think about your future before getting yourself into troubles like this? Anyway, I am letting you go this time. Go with Mr Agrawal and complete some paperwork."

'*Vijay Purohit.*' I read his name on the plate. He was really a nice man.

"Thank a lot, sir," I said in a teary voice.

"Make sure it does not happen again," he warned.

He was really kind and understanding. Thankfully he was not a member of the Anti-lovers' Association. Some police guys are active members of that. I wrote an application stating my mistake and reassuring that I would not repeat it in future. I felt relieved.

"Son, we recommended your case to S.H.O. That is why he let you go scot free," Mr Agrawal said.

"Thank you, sir," I faked a smile.

'You are the bastard who made me suffer all this,' I thought.

"Today is your girlfriend's birthday and we prevented you from going to jail, so where is our treat?"

"Sir, how much do you need?" I was humble in my tone

but not in feelings. He was surprised by my straight-forwardness.

"4,000. We need to give, larger share to S.H.O.," the other policeman said.

In India there is a protocol for everything. The most interesting being that of corruption. I walked to a nearest ATM with them. Aditi's birthday cost me a total sum of 8,000 and gave me some of the nastiest moments of my life. I reached my room at 2:15 a.m. There were 50 missed calls. All from the birthday girl. I called up her.

"Hi," I said with a deep breath.

"Where have you been? Why did those policemen take you away? What happened?" she unleashed the chain of questions.

"Wait, wait," I drank a glass of water and started the whole story. She was bemused to know everything.

Joker's Jottings

Buy the permission to loiter around a girls' hostel from the police. And those with burnt pockets, please buy gifts for your sweethearts from a chor bazaar. It saves your ass.

Guys, this one from Naidu: stop watching porn for long hours. It's injurious to health..

Chapter Eleven

The Perfect Humiliation

My phone rang. I travelled back to the present.

"Hello."

"Are you ready?" Bharti on the other side asked.

"Almost."

"The whole crew is waiting for you. Be at Gate 2 within five minutes."

"Okay."

Our bus was to leave for the airport at 9 p.m. I hurried up.

Bharti was already sitting in the bus.

"How are your legs?"

"They're fine."

"Hi," I waved my hand at the other crew members sitting in back rows. I took the empty seat beside Bharti. Sitting in the adjacent row were Tina and Yash, our only competitors left. After the last mudslinging episode, we were not on amiable terms.

"Is everything allright?" Tina tried to strike a conversation.

"Yeah, how are you both?" I gave a grin.

"Absolutely fine."

"Have you guys ever been to Varanasi?" Yash asked.

"No," I said.

"Let us hope everything goes perfect."

"Yeah, fingers crossed," I signalled.

"Bloody scoundrels," I whispered to Bharti.

"Mr Jitender Singh, come to the cabin," Vineet sir announced in a high-pitched voice.

Vineet sir was the coordinator-cum-manager of the show. Jitenderji was a senior crew member. For the last few months they had been the family, so I knew almost all of them.

"I crossed the mark of 1,000," Bharti nudged me.

"What?" I exclaimed.

"Inbox is flooded with messages and the flow continues. What about you?"

"Crossed only 500."

"Look at your face," she giggled.

"Bharti, are you not nervous?"

She looked into my eyes and held my hands. "Believe in yourself and have faith in God. We are almost there."

I smiled. I felt really on top of the world.

We reached the airport at 9:15 p.m. eventually. The secretive talk going between Vineet sir and Jitenderji unfolded into a full-fledged drama. Only the location shifted from the driver's cabin to the lounge. We kept observing everything curiously. I was too lost in the scene.

"Were you out of your mind while doing this?" Vineet sir was furious.

"Sir, believe me I did not pass on info to anyone," Jitenderji was literally on his knees.

Another five minutes and Jitenderji was given a pink slip. My sympathy was with Jitenderji. It appeared like that the poor guy was thrown out unreasonably. The incident took me back to the lanes of memories, where something similar had happened with me.

Eight months ago, January 30th, this year.

I was standing in Prof. Khanna's chamber. My eyes were red, my head was down and tears were falling on my shoes. I held a letter in my hands which turned my world topsy-turvy. The letter said:

Dear Mr Abhi Sharma

We are really disappointed with your wrongdoings. You let the Institute's reputation down. On account of the grave indisciplined act, you are expelled from Apex Institute.

A detailed letter will be sent to your guardian...

Twice I tried to cross that, but I failed in reading further. How would my parents react to this? The thought made me jittery. I had brought a bad name to everyone associated with me. This ill-fated volcano erupted six hours ago.

Exactly six hours ago I was sitting in a classroom of Toppers' Institute, the same class in which Aditi studied. It was the last day of the one-week-long revision class of rotational mechanics. Attending lectures in an institute where you do not belong is always a thrilling experience. I remember how nervous I was on the first day. But once Aditi accompanied me past the guard to the classroom, I turned fearless. Prof. K.K. was really hilarious. His tips and pedagogy made solving sums easier. Everything was running smoothly till that pretty lady from the administrative section interrupted the class. She muttered something to Prof. K.K. Her hands indicated that she was explaining something to him. After a short while she turned towards the class. "Okay. I will not take much of your time. I have come here to collect your IIT-JEE application number," she paused for a while and continued, "This practice is done to track your results. Since the session expires by the start of March and the results are announced in May, so it's essential for us to keep the records."

Girls in the front rows started sharing the required info with the bespectacled lady. Sitting in the fourth row, my legs were trembling and palms were wet. I was not a student of Toppers' Institute and what if she asked me about my identity.

"Yes! You in the blue."

I stood up. "Madam, I forgot my application number. I will positively submit to you tomorrow," I formulated the best possible excuse to escape. I looked at Aditi. She appeared more worried than me.

"Okay! Tell me your roll number."

Now I was caught with pants down. Telling a lie would make things complicated. I thought.

"I am not a student of this institute," I closed my eyes while spilling the truth.

There was a loud uproar in the class. All eyes were glued to me as if I was either a joker or a terrorist.

Every face was curious. I was immediately escorted to the principal's office by Prof. K.K. and that lady. The counterpart of Prof. Khanna at Toppers was much similar to him in physique. Often the size of the stomach is proportional to the chair one occupies. The lady narrated the whole scene to the principal.

"So boy, do you have any explanation?" the principal asked.

"Sir, I will not tell any lie to you. I was very weak at mechanics. When I heard that Prof. K.K. was conducting a revision class, I could not stop myself. Every student in Kota knows that he is the best at mechanics."

No one hates his flatterers. Everyone in the room looked satisfied with my explanation. They could gauge the honesty in it.

"Which institute?" A mollified principal asked.

"I am from Apex."

"So Apex does not have quality teachers? What do you say?" The principal gave a sarcastic look.

Apex and Toppers' were known for their age-old rivalry. The race to the top slot always gets dirtier.

"No sir, It is just...," I stopped and bowed my head in shame. Saying anything in that regard was not wise.

"Do you know, you can be sent behind the bars for this grave wrongdoing?"

"I am sorry but my intentions were not wrong. Please forgive me."

This was second time that I was in a situation where I was getting a warning of being sent to jail. That too in the same month! First it was Aditi's birthday, then her institute. Perhaps some element of black magic had made a tragic entry into my love life.

"This boy appears sincere in his studies. Though he is involved in all this mischief, but he is committed to his goals. I think we should be moderate with him," a till now silent Prof. K.K. tilted the balance in my favour. He found a sycophant in me and nobody wants to see one's sycophant in trouble.

"Do you have any friend who helped you in this?" the principal asked in a stricter tone.

"No, sir," I lied.

"Okay, you do one thing...," he stopped and started thinking something.

He looked at me as if I was a part of the enemy's espionage.

"Submit a confession letter stating your guilt, purpose of coming into these premises and agreeing to any future punitive action awarded to you."

"Yes sir," I had no other choice.

Five hours later, I got a ring from Apex Institute. I was asked to reach immediately Prof. Khanna's office. I had an inkling that it was related to Toppers' episode.

The administrative building appeared like a court where I was going to be convicted. Unfortunately, Prof. Sen, the physics teacher who taught mechanics to our class was already waiting for me in the office. The predator always has

to wait for the prey. Another senior administrative official was also present in the room.

"Welcome, Mr Sharma," the wicked smile of Prof. Sen made me nervous.

"You scoundrel, what is this?"

A furious Prof. Khanna handed me a copy of the confession letter which I had submitted to the principal at Toppers' Institute. The bloody principal had used me in the mudslinging game between the two coaching tycoons.

"Sir, I am really sorry for that," I avoided his eyes.

"Do you even know what this means?"

I preferred to keep silent.

"Firstly, it puts a question mark on our teaching capability. Secondly, it shows that our students are insincere and mischievous. Thirdly, it implies that Toppers' is better than Apex. God knows what would happen if this news gets leaked to the media?" Prof. Khanna was loud and violent.

"I am pretty sure that the local media will find about it and Topper's will love to leak the news."

Sen alias Devil always knew how to make things worse.

"Then it will be absolute havoc" the other senior official said.

The court martial continued for half an hour. For most part of the time I was just a listener—listener to their abuses and villainous titles they conferred on me. Their intense scorn and hatred in words made me feel like a rapist. My face, eyes, ears, cheeks, almost everything thing except my hair turned red. Red is a colour of shame. And, also of love. For them their reputation was at stake. In the Indian society, honour lies at the top of the hierarchy's priority. Even human life comes next to it.

After a proper humiliation, I was asked to leave the chamber with an expulsion letter. I was thrown out of the Apex Institute. What an achievement! Ironically it was the 30th of January, Martyr's Day.

Next day the newspaper did publish the whole news in detail. To protect my identity they used a false name. *Student expelled from Apex Institute.* The headline said of the honour I brought to my family.

Very soon they would be getting the letter from the Institute intimating them everything. The thought bothered me a lot. I was too coward to tell them about it. Whenever I imagined the to-be wrath of my parents, goosebumps and sweat covered my body. For the first time in my life, I was ashamed of myself. Hopelessness was ubiquitous in my life.

"It's really unfortunate," Rohan broke the silence. Rohan, Vivek and Naidu were on a consolation visit to me. Since their arrival, they did not say a word except a mute 'hello'. It is hard to start the discourse in front of a victim.

"I do not know how my parents will react to this?" I did

not care for my expulsion as much as I did for its impression on my parents.

"Do not worry for that," Vivek said.

I gave him a please-explain-to-me look.

"They will never come to know," he took out an envelope from his pocket and continued. "This was the letter to be sent to your parents. We somehow managed to get its possession from a clerk. Now do not worry for anything."

"What?" I was startled. "How did you manage that?"

More than half of my agony vanished. If my parents remained unaware of my expulsion, then there was no big deal with it. Fuck the bloody expulsion. I grabbed the letter and tore it apart without any delay. I felt lighter and better.

"You did not tell how?" I asked.

"Everything sells. Just show the money," Vivek said.

"Thanks. I owe a lot to you guys."

We huddled together. With their hands on my shoulders, I felt stronger. They were really true friends. Love put me into trouble and friendship rescued me from it. I assume that is a common phenomenon with a large chunk of the junta. So the moral of the story is—bring good friends home before you turn ultra passionate for a girl.

Meanwhile, Aditi deprived herself of food, water and sleep. Her non-stop teary melodrama continued in full swing. Through Riya, I even came to know about her swollen eyes. I called her up. "Aditi, what is all this?"

"It is my entire fault," she was sobbing.

"Okay, stop this nonsense. Why did you not take food?" I spilled out my anger. Instead of being adaptive to the situation, she engaged herself in *tamasha.*

"No, sweetheart. Let me punish myself. I deserve it."

"Oh, come on. Everything is fixed. It is all right. Let us forget what happened, like a bad dream. It was not your fault. Rather my bad luck."

"Really!" she exclaimed and continued. "You are really the best guy in this whole world."

"Yeah, I know. But now I am really starving. Let us eat out."

"Me too."

"Let us go to the Durbar," I took a sigh of relief.

I took her on my way to the restaurant.

"Twenty-four hours before I was thrown out of my institute with perfect humiliation and now I am having yummy food at a posh restaurant."

"All for your love!" Aditi held my hands tightly.

How true!

Joker's Jottings

Jugaad *rocks! By the way, have you ever tasted expulsion? Comes with a price but it tastes of freedom and makes you more popular among girls.*

Sometimes teachers are the root of all evils. Or love? So make a fan community of your teachers and professors on social sites. Learn some tactics of buttering with an I-love-licking attitude.

Chapter Twelve

Shock, Intimacy & Betrayal

There is an old saying that you cannot avert what destiny has in store for you. Two days later, a phone call woke me up at 10 in morning.

"Hi, Papa!"

"Is it true, Abhi?"

"What?"

"Have you been expelled from the institute?"

The morning laziness and sleepiness vanished with a jolt. The thunderstorm finally struck. Shock, shock, shock. Absolutely unexpected!

"Yes," I spoke like a lamb.

"Disgusting, what the hell did you do?"

The disappointment in my father's voice was evident.

"Papa, I am really sorry. But believe me, I did nothing wicked. I was caught attending a lecture at another institute."

"Well, I really do not feel like talking to you. Talk to your mother," he sounded disheartened. Making your parents disappointed is a risk not well taken.

"Hello, Mom. Do not be upset. I am really sorry for what has happened."

"You should be," she too was displeased. Why not? After all the laurels I brought them was worth it.

"Please do not be so angry with me. I am emotionally devastated. I need your support."

An inevitable truth of life is that your parents always love you. That is why even God has been compared to them. They were flabbergasted, but they felt the pain and guilt in my voice.

Half an hour later the picture became crystal clear. A simultaneous letter was sent to my local guardian, who indeed was Jaiswal Uncle. I destroyed the one supposed to be sent to my parents but the other one was overlooked by Vivek and party. They missed the letter and it screwed everything that was put back on the resilient mode, with great effort. The other alarming thing was my parents who were coming to Kota within two days. They already announced it and were adamant. Two days passed smoothly in planning a drama with Vivek, Rohan, Naidu, Aditi and Riya. Finally it was show time.

"Hi, Uncle! Hi, Aunty!" everybody exchanged handshakes with Papa and Mom.

"You resemble Sheetal. Beautiful and gorgeous! Just like her," my mother was very happy to see Aditi.

"Uncle, I must say that what happened with Abhi was unfortunate. It was sheer bad luck." There was a good thing about Rohan that he exuded conviction while speaking.

"But what he did was absolutely wrong," Papa said.

"There is another side to this story. The grass is not as green as it appears. The teaching quality in the city has fallen. At times we feel neglected. In such a case rushing to a teacher like Prof. K.K. becomes indispensable. All Abhi wanted was to learn mechanics from the maestro," Riya delivered her part marvellously.

As planned everything was going alright.

"In fact, there were also other students in the class who were outsiders," Aditi quipped.

Every bit of drama was being orchestrated with great care and precaution.

"Even I attend lectures at a place where I do not belong to."

Like me, Vivek was a plausible liar.

My mother and father looked at him with astonishment.

"Son, beware. You could be in danger," my mother warned.

"No, Aunty. The risk is worth the concepts and tips I get. Besides, I feel cheated at Apex. They just look after a few top batches."

"Amidst the growing rivalry between the two institutes, Abhi has been made scapegoat," Naidu remarked. Everybody was assigned their part.

"I can understand your concern with the decline in educational standards. It is true. Absolutely. But the big question is what will he do now? I mean no classes to attend. Then what?" Papa put up a question for the drama party.

"Self-study. It is the best option. By the way the session is going to expire by the end of this month. So he does not have much to lose," Rohan spilled out the nuggets of wisdom.

"Yes, he is right," I supported.

My God and Goddess looked convinced. I felt happy. Papa and Mom took all of us to a restaurant. We all relished food together.

All this had a positive impact on my studies. The bulb of wisdom finally started glowing in me. Importance of a sound preparation and eventually good results occupied my brain cells. For most of the time I stayed in the room, insulated from outside and dedicated to my subjects. The one who falls knows rising better.

Four days after my parents left, I got an unusual visitor at my room.

"Hello, Abhi *bhaiya*, how are you?" I was taken by surprise by Raju *bhaiya's* visit.

"Hi *bhaiya*! I am fine. You here?"

"Yeah, you were not coming to the shop. I thought maybe something is wrong with your health."

I was a regular at his tea-stall but I had not gone there once since the last one week.

"Nothing wrong. Health is fine. Busy in studies."

"Oh, come on. Do not befool me. I know you very well. Anything wrong with Aditi?"

"Not at all," I laughed and continued, "I am really touched by your gesture." Being studious didn't go well with my persona. Well it happens so with a majority.

"Then come to the shop in evening."

"Okay," I nodded.

I was always good at social dynamics. Perhaps that is why I had a list of well, wishers. Indeed man is a social animal.

Three things held priority in my to-do list. Valentine's day, test on 15th and 17th februray.

Seventeenth was the date on which Sheetal Aunty was coming to Kota. Aditi was very excited and so was I.

We did not plan big for Valentine's Day, not because I

had a test one day later, but as a precaution to the moral brigade *tamasha*. I preferred to meet Aditi just for few minutes and that too after dusk. It was better to keep a safe distance from trouble. A lesson I sincerely learnt.

On the pleasant Sunday morning of 17th, my to-be mother-in-law arrived at Kota.

"*Mom wants to meet you. Come to hotel Holiday Inn, 205. Waiting eagerly. Love you.*"

The SMS escalated the excitement within me. Shaving, bathing, putting on a chic dress, I did everything properly. Bathing for me was a weekly event which I had already performed two days ago. But the need of the hour was that I appear elegant and classy. Anything to impress mother-in-law.

"Hello, Aunty."

"Here comes the prince. Come son, come."

Sheetal Aunty embraced me. She looked much younger than her age. Aditi's face was an absolute photocopy of her mother. I liked the well-groomed bun on Aunty's head. It went well with her persona.

"So how are you?"

"Fine. You look so young, aunty."

"Oh, thanks."

"I have heard a lot about you from Mummy. She talks a lot about you."

"Yeah, we really had a great time in college. Anyway it has been a long time since I met your mother."

She offered some *laddoos* and other homemade snacks.

"Thanks."

"Does she study properly?" she pointed towards Aditi.

"Absolutely. She is an intelligent girl. She is going to rock."

Aditi winked at me and giggled, "Mom, let us go out for a movie and then..."

"But first promise me that you are going to fare well in your Board exams. I believe that you are not sincere enough in Board preparations."

"Do not worry, Aunty. Board exams are nothing but a cakewalk. She will surely excel," I had the experience.

"Yes Mom, he is right," Aditi supported.

"Okay, then you people enjoy television and I will take a quick shower. Then we will go for a movie after lunch," Sheetal Aunty helped herself to the bathroom.

"There is no need of being so sober in front of Mom."

"Really," I pulled Aditi towards myself. Aunty's absence from the room gave us the much needed privacy. We both longed for that.

"There was something which I could not do on 14th."

I said and kissed her rosy lips. It was velvety. My hands fondled her hair that skimmed her back and stopped at her

lascivious hunkers. Impulsively she took her hands from my neck to down in my pants. She touched it. I felt the volcanic surge within my body. It was irresistible.

"Let us do it," she said.

"Are you crazy? Your mother can come anytime. She is going to kill me if she finds out."

"Come on. She takes at least half an hour in the bathroom. It is her habit. Do not worry."

I looked at the watch. We had already lost five minutes. I pushed her to the bed. With every cloth we took off, the temperature of the room soared. The ambience was getting hotter and raunchier. The slower the undressing the steamier it gets.

"You look ravishing."

"And you tempting," she retorted.

We left no corners of our bodies unexplored. The passion was driving us crazy. I unhooked her bra. Mount Everests turned into Nanga Parbats. I kissed them. The journey from 69 to 96 was erotically salty and weary. After the Ranthambore episode, Vivek gifted me the rubber. I always kept it in my wallet.

"Wow, you always kept yourself prepared," Aditi was taken by surprise by my possession.

"Precaution, darling. I do not want to see you with a big stomach."

"Shut up."

With every push I exerted, her eyes sparkled with sensuality. Aditi's hands held a firm grip on the pillow. Her moans made me feel like a lion.

"Why are you crying?" Tears in her eyes made me pause for a while.

"No sweetheart, it is the pleasure of the pain. I love you, my sugarplum."

Eleven days before the Board exams, we consummated our relation in a situation which was unexpected, unprecedented and incredibly filmy. Sheetal Aunty could never figure out what happened in her pseudo presence. I can never forget those 10 minutes of out-of-world pleasure. Supreme happiness. Neither can Aditi. I felt some kind of divinity while making love with Aditi. Perhaps sex is a physical interpretation of divine communion of two souls. Maybe that is why more people go for communion with more than one soul. Positive attitude, eh? Sheetal Aunty brought luck for me. The amatory experience could not have been possible without her support. Blind and secret. My lucky mascot!

One day later she went back to Dehradun. I wished if only she could have stayed a little longer.

March passed like a march-past, speedily and rhythmically! Aditi had her exams scheduled at regular intervals. I enrolled in a correspondence course of a different institute which

included an All India Test series plus Genius package. The whole of Kota was coloured in competitive tinge. The city's soul inspired and motivated each of its inhabitants to work hard. Vivek, Naidu, Rohan and everybody else engaged themselves in honing the concepts. Ten hours a day became a habit for me. Everything else took a backseat. IIT joint entrance exam was to be held on 13th April. The harder I studied the more confident I felt. Then something happened. Tragic and devastating! April 1st changed our lives. That was the day when destiny fooled us. A bitter reality of life met me head on. A loud knock at my door disturbed the hardly-three-hour old sleep. It was 8:15 in the morning.

"You," Naidu stood at my door. My eyes were still half open. Leaving aside a few exceptions, I never saw Naidu awake so early in the morning. He was panting and looked agitated.

"Rohan is no more."

"Hey, I am no fool. I know it's April 1st."

I gave a grin. I knew Naidu was a brilliant prankster.

"I am serious. Last night he committed suicide," he choked. Tears started rolling out on his cheeks. He put his head on my shoulder and started sighing heavily.

It could not be a joke. The air of my room turned grim.

"But why?" I felt my vocal cord paralysed. Rohan was no more alive. Hard to believe, harder to digest! Numbness filled my brain.

"Don't know."

We both cried. Louder and louder.

When we reached Rohan's room, the police had already taken away his body for the post mortem. For us, the Hiroshima and Nagasaki happened the same day. We loved him and now we lost him. A large gathering of students and neighbours packed the whole area. Rohan's landlord, who was surrounded by journalists and cameramen, looked aghast at the happening. He signalled Vivek, Naidu and me to come towards him.

"They were his closest friends in the city," he introduced us to the journalists. All cameras focused on us. That ill-fated morning we were being made the part of breaking news. The news that really broke us!

"What do you think was the reason behind Rohan's suicide?" one of the journalists asked.

"Well we don't really know. Everything was all right. We least expected the tragedy. It is out of the blue," I sobbed while I spoke.

"How was Rohan at studies and was he of reserved nature?" another query came from the mediaman. I didn't feel like answering that question. My silence forced Vivek to make a reply.

"He was meritorious and sincere at his studies. He was a

nice person and a very helping friend. I miss him so much. I don't know...I am at a loss for words," he choked. Who won't be in such a situation?

"Do you think it has something to do with a girl or some family pressure?"

That was it. The question made me lose my control.

"How could you guys be so shallow and cold? We are no puppets to add *masala* to your breaking news. We have lost someone who was close to our heart and you all are digging the shit out of us. Please excuse us," I walked away from those *masala*-hungry hunters. Naidu and Vivek followed me. I could not condone the media's callousness. Any profession is incomplete without heart. Power, influence and competition have made media corrupt. Anger accompanied the sadness inside me.

Loss is like love; it never fades away. You cry in both. Love is heaven, loss is hell. Life is either love or loss. No middle path. You love, you lose again you love and lose. Rohan's betrayal was an eternal loss.

He left a note for us.

Dear Slayers,

'Slayers' was our team's name in counter strike. The team which had now lost its vigour.

I love you all. I know my departure would come as a shock to you. Believe me: the decision was even more difficult for me. I was entangled and my fate kept betraying me. I am sorry but I cannot bear the depression. Sorry for the betrayal.

May God give you the power to heal the burns!

Yours Rohan.

Peer pressure. That was the reason behind all this. But we were his peers. How could we be responsible? The picture was slightly different. For the last two months, Rohan had been more diligent and sincere than one could imagine. Unfortunately the same could not convert into his results. His percentage in All India Tests did not improve. He was quite hopeful but the things simply did not fall in places. Sadly, the drastic step! But he performed better than thousands of other students. Why did he not think of that? Why did he not discuss his feelings with us? He left many questions unanswered. Making a career the hinge of life can ruin it. For two days we did not eat anything. Our hunger died with Rohan. The shock was not sinking in. I stayed at Vivek's place. Loneliness haunted me. We supported each other, we cried together and we missed Rohan's presesnce. Ten days later, we had the IIT entrance exam. The crucial point of our career was approaching. Everything was pell-mell. Back in January, Rohan invited me to shift to his place. Had I done that, I could have saved a friend. A true friend! Pressure is always painful. Bloody peer pressure.

Joker's Jottings

Help your friends in conning their parents. It's the dharma *of adolescence.*

Make sure your wallet has the rubber. This contributes in fighting AIDS and overpopulation.

Preoccupy your life with several noble things like smoking, drinking, flirting and partying to avoid depression. I hope I could have given this advice to Rohan. Shut your mind and start masti *and* bakchodi. *Pressure and worries? Kick them hard.*

Chapter Thirteen

What's Immoral? Stupid!

One hour had already passed since the flight took off for Varanasi. My cheeks felt moist. I felt someone wringing my heart. Rohan was a dear friend. His absence meant a lot.

"Hey, what happened?" Bharti lent a hand to wipe the tears on my face.

"Memories," I choked.

"Something you would like to share."

"A good friend of mine committed suicide before IIT entrance exam. Just missing him."

"How sad! I can understand," she held a firm grip on my hand.

"Eat this. You will feel better," she offered me a chocolate.

Bharti was really a nice and understanding girl. I was really lucky to have her by my side.

"You never told me how did you land at this show?"

"What do you want to know?" I was always protective about my past.

"Everything, like I have told about myself," she said.

"Okay. But do stop me if you get bored," I said.

"Don't worry. I love listening."

"Wow! I can't imagine that a singer is saying that," I bantered.

I bared my heart to Bharti. Everything! The journey in flashback again stopped at Rohan's betrayal. This time there were no tears but I looked agitated.

"Now I understand your pain," she said.

By the time we had reached Varanasi and were on our way to the hotel, it was past midnight and everyone except us appeared tired and sleepy. Tina and Yash kept looking at us intermittently. I knew they were too curious to know about what we were talking about. Rivalry. They knew that we had greater chances of winning. Better performance and cleaner image in the eyes of the public was our strength. Jealous—they always felt of us.

"So what happened after that?" Bharti pushed me back to the lanes of memories.

It was the IIT entrance exam day. The pattern of questions was a surprise for all the candidates. Nobody had expected the way it turned out to be. But I was not at all surprised; it was too less to surprise me. I had the experience of the greater ones. Within hours of the exam, various coaching institutes came up with the solution and expected cut-offs and the sundry nonsense. I did not bother to check them. I knew I had given my best shot and I did not want to anticipate anything. Expectations often lead to miseries. In my case, always! Please try to keep the page of expectations blank in life. It helps. Everybody talked of cut-offs. Rank-projection gossips became the hobby of the geeky *phodus*. The examination season was taking its colour. I had two more left—AIEEE and BITSAT. AIEEE was in the last week of April and BITSAT was scheduled in the second week of May. In between I had to move to Delhi where my BITSAT centre was assigned. Luckily, Naidu too got the same allocation. Vivek was not eligible to appear in BITSAT. The poor guy could not score 80 per cent in his 12th Boards. He left Kota after AIEEE. Naidu and I went to bid him goodbye. We three sang two songs before Vivek's train left Kota. *Surat niraali, man ki tu kaali.....jhooth mat bol ki kala kauwa kaat khayega...*The Punjabi hit was followed by a soft rock...*Leaving on a jet plane....* On first song, we rejoiced and the second one made us nostalgic. It was Rohan's favorite.

The first one was a salute to the charming city and second one was an ode to a dear friend. I remember, the whole compartment looked at us amusingly. For them we were unleashed jokers of some circus. Yes, the circus of friendship, *masti* and a lot more. We belonged to that.

"When are you leaving?"

"Day after tomorrow," Aditi said.

"Sweetheart, perhaps this is the last time we are sitting here."

Chambal Garden would always remain afresh in the hearts of whosoever has fallen in love at Kota. Love at Kota is incomplete without Chambal Garden. My head rested on Aditi's lap. I took her hand and kissed it.

"I don't want to go. I wish to stay here. With you, my Kohinoor!" she said.

"I know but we are at the crossroad…"

"I really don't know what is going to happen in the next two months. There is a qualm inside my head," she interrupted me.

"Results?"

"And Admission too," she added.

"IIT?"

"Not really but even if I don't qualify, I am not going to waste one more year for further preparations. I want to be in college at the earliest."

"Great thoughts! Yearning for college fun! Don't worry, you'll get it, " I kissed on her forehead.

"Do you know, last night Riya kept crying for hours?"

"Vivek factor?" she nodded.

"So are you going to cry for me?" I asked.

"No sweetheart because you stay here," she took my hand to her heart. I pressed her boobs. She retaliated by pinching me in the neck.

"You naughty! Don't do it next time. Remember, if you have my boobs then I have your balls."

"I am going to miss it," I winked at her. She mocked me.

Day after that Aditi went back to Dehradun. Within 12 hours of her departure, we had exchanged more than 50 SMSes. *'I miss u'* became our new slogan. The love story which was impregnated in Kota moved towards a different juncture where the love was the distance between us. Months of dating and romance. Alas! No more. The big question was that when would I get a chance to meet her again. We left it on time.

I scored a double century in BITSAT and Naidu scored only a century. Had I done it in cricket, I would have been treated like a demigod but even with a score of 200, there was no chance of getting admission into BITS, Pilani.

"I hate online tests. Why do they show the score immediately? It sucks," Naidu was freaked out by his performance.

"Don't be impatient. Two more to come."

"Yeah. Anyway I want to forget all this. Let's go for some movie."

"Okay."

"Are you a virgin?" Naidu asked me just after the movie started. I was amused by the timing of his query.

"Yes," I lied.

"Then let us go to them."

"Who?"

"Prostitutes."

"What?"

The movie screening in front of us dealt with the subject of passion and infidelity. Perhaps it tickled the steamy emotions in Naidu.

"Dude, I am already 19 and I have still not fucked a single girl. Sometimes I feel too tempted and restless."

We left the movie hall and returned back to our hotel. Somewhere inside my mind, I was also excited about the idea.

* * *

"So did you guys go to prostitutes?" How would you feel if a girl asks this question of you? Shameless! Exactly what I felt at that time!

"Don't you think we should have some chocolates before we start on that?"

“Sure, my pleasure!”I took out two pieces of chocolate and offered one to Bharti. Eating chocolates makes you feel better. Then I started again from where I left.

We left the movie hall and returned back to our hotel. Naidu contacted a pimp and he agreed to send two girls. We went in two separate rooms. I had tasted it once and like any normal guy wanted to have more. There are few things in the world that are never bad even if they are in excess. At one point of time I thought of Aditi, fidelity, trust but lust inside me overpowered everything. Lust rusts the wisdom. Though I had seen some blurred snaps of prostitutes shown in media and except for a few glances I got on my visit to Chor Bazaar in Kota, I had never been fortunate enough to meet anyone of them. I must say if you believe in breaking fences then go for it. The much-waited knock finally arrived. The girl clad in jeans and top was barely twenty-years old. I signalled her to come inside and sit on the bed.

“My sexy hero, tonight I am going to take you to the heaven,” she tweaked my cheek and winked. I was taken aback by the boldness. What a commitment to the profession!

“What’s your name?”

“Does it matter to you?”

“Well your boobs are like footballs. They are appetising,” I tried to strike a naughty cord. What I had

heard from some people was that prostitutes have expertise at talking naughtier things. I thought of starting from there. The prelude to foreplay is in getting dirty and nasty.

"Oye *chutiye*, this is the way you going to treat me. Just talking! Your generation is so *harami* and *tharki*. You seem to be an exception. Come here and I'll show you."

With a flash she caught hold of my jeans and unzipped it. The testosterone inside me fired high to sky. Few minutes of fondling and the snake became impatient to come outside. She pulled my underpants down the knees. Her lips started playing vigorously with the lollipop. Her one hand caressed it and the other rested on my thighs. My hands clawed her footballs. If I said so then I truly meant it. I unbuttoned her jeans and took her undies off. Unlike me, she had no pubic hair. The ground was plain and smooth. I let my tongue perform jerky movements at the alluring and coveted hole for which every guy yearns since his puberty. I tickled her G-spot. Fingers followed the tongue. The fluid started coming out of her genitals. She was finally enjoying the orgasm.

"Fuck me hard! Fuck me! Come inside." Her moans grew louder with repetitive invitation to enter her smoothness. I kept her invitation for later and placed my snake at her cleavage. The snake was as straight as teak. The warmth of teak tempted her to press the snake between her boobs.

"*Saale tu to bahut garam launda hain,*" she remarked. I bent to her face to have the first smooch of the encounter. She was a treasure trove of pleasure. When the time came to share my warmth inside her body, she turned around to let me play the dog. She played the bitch. What an awesome bitch she was!

The whole night, the goddess of Kamasutra tutored me with her erogenous skills. I had never known a better yoga teacher. The whole exercise cost me 2,000 bucks.

Next morning I did not feel all right. The lust had faded away and the guilt was dominant. Did I cheat Aditi? Why did it happen? I felt like a demon. What if Aditi had done the same? I shivered.

"It was awesome. Is it not?" Naidu came to my room with a coffee mug. He looked happy.

"Naidu, please don't tell anyone about this."

"*Saale* why would I?" He saw the guilt in my eyes.

"By the way you look so tired. Was she electrifying?" he bantered.

"Thunderstorm," I smiled and continued, "I don't know why but I am feeling bad for Aditi." The expression on my face changed like a politician's loyalty.

"Don't worry. One time is absolutely fine. She will never come to know."

"Still..."

"Still what? There is no point in being sad or guilty about it. Just forget it."

"Was it not immoral?"

"What immoral? Stupid. Is not polygamy immoral? In ancient India, kings used to have more than one wife. It's perception. If a lot of bad things can be practiced in the name of culture, then what we did last night was absolutely okay. Don't behave like hypocrites."

"And this is the land of Kamasutra," I kicked away the guilt.

"Absolutely."

We were no philosophers but what I knew for certain was that we were irrationally justified. Naidu took a flight for Chandigarh at noon. He had lost his virginity and was proud of that. I gave a visit to Shruti before boarding the train for Jamshedpur. She was hale and hearty. A bit more! I met Anuj. Her new boyfriend. Prateek was replaced. These days relations change too quickly. I found that she had become more artificial. Nowadays the hardest thing to do is being you. Everyone is masquerading. She was no longer herself. The same scene was with me. Alas! We are in a world where nothing is permanent. Nothing.

In one year of my stay at Kota, I underwent a roller-coaster ride. Love *sutras*, Friendship *fundas*, mechanics *mantras* almost everything pleasant as well as nasty. I had visited every shade of passion.

Back at home it was celebration time. Meeting friends, relatives, neighbours kept me engaged. Eating home-made food was a heavenly pleasure. My fights with Richa over TV remote resumed. Richa, my sister, was two years elder to me but I never called her *Didi*. the reason, we grew as friends in childhood. Perhaps this was also the reason why she always tried to be bossy with me. Every time she tried, I resisted. She was doing her graduation from a very reputed college in Jamshedpur and to my mother's delight, she was the topper of her class. I always wondered about her academic feat for she was not a bookworm type. On the contrary, she was exceptionally good at singing and other extra-curricular activities. I had missed her a lot. She was almost in tears the day I arrived.

But soon the festivity ended. The bugle blew. Results were announced on May 30th. Neither did I qualify in IIT exam nor was I eligible for admission to any NITs. Vivek, Naidu, Riya and Aditi joined me in the failed bandwagon. But every one of them had a silver lining. Vivek and Naidu had applied for some state engineering colleges. They had applied at a dozen places. They got a chance in one of the lesser known colleges. Riya had qualified in the West Bengal Engineering exam and got a seat in computer science engineering department through state quota. Though

Aditi could not make it to any engineering college, but unexpectedly she scored a brilliant 93 percent in Class XII Board exams. She was no fool to miss a chance in top colleges of Delhi.

As far as I was concerned, I lost my self-esteem. Does darkness taste? Yes. Bitter than death! That was the time in my life when I feared looking at the mirror for it showed despair. I yearned for light but it kept moving away. It finally flickered, with a phone call.

"Hello. Is this Mr Abhi?"

"Yes."

"I am calling from M4U TV. You would be glad to know that you have been selected for India's Musical Jodi Show. You are required to report to our Mumbai office by 15th June. We will send you an invitation letter shortly. Good luck."

Is it for real? For a minute, I was boggled. What is this? I was confused. An unexpected surprise!

It all started in Delhi after my BITS admission test. Naidu and I happened to pass by an auditorium where a lot of junta were shouting slogans. From the banner there, we came to know that auditions for a music reality show were going on inside. The posters asked dancing and singing enthusiasts to turn up and prove their mettle. I always had a special interest in dance. Given the fabulous track record of my dancing dexterity I was tempted to give a try. Even Naidu tried to shake his legs. He did, but badly. About selection, we were told that once the auditions get completed in all metro cities, the organising team will sort out the finalists. Two days later, I got an invitation letter from M4U TV. It said of the terms and conditions of the show. The format of the show was a little different. Top 10 dancers and singers were selected among thousands of aspirants. Ten pairs were made, each comprising a singer and a dancer of the opposite sex. I was in top 10 dancers selected across the country. At last I had something to be proud about. I was excited. I needed a reason to run away from home, a reason to forget my failures. I wanted a chance to prove that I too can be an achiever. I wanted my self-esteem back.

"And that is how I got to meet a wonderful person like you."

"It is too filmy. Is it not?" Bharti asked.

"Yes."

I met Bharti on 16th June during the orientation programme for the contestants. If I was a good dancer, then she was a better singer.

"Let us sit inside," I said. We were in the hotel balcony for last 40 minutes. I looked at the watch. It was 3:00 in the morning.

"So, how is Aditi?"

"We have not talked for last one month. She thinks that I am involved with you." On the show I was romantically linked with Bharti a couple of times. People around us said that we had a sizzling chemistry.

"Oh, I am really sorry for being an eyesore of your love life. In fact I also got some queries regarding our affair."

"This channel can do anything to gain TRPs."

"The underbelly of the TV world is really dirty. No values, only profits. Do you remember my birthday?"

"Of course I do," I said. On Bharti's birthday I gifted her bouquet of roses. The production guys somehow captured the scene. In the next episode, it was telecast with a romantic tinge. Even our friendly embrace was shown with a love song in the background. The whole country watched it. From that day we both became beware of the camera. A camera has an amazing power to frame the truth. Dangerously deceptive!

"Abhi, can I ask you a question?" there was an abrupt change in Bharti's tone.

"Yeah, sure. Go ahead."

"Do you like me?"

"Yes, of course. You are a nice girl and you have been so sweet to me."

"Don't you think that we make a great off-screen pair?"

I was dazzled by her question. I had never thought over it. I didn't say anything. We were sitting on the sofa. She glided her way to me. And there she bent over me and glued a kiss on my cheek. I had not had it for a long time, but I least expected it from her. I was left gaping at her. I was in a quandary. We had been together for three months. Three months is a long time. Besides, Bharti had a sensual figure, the one which arouses libido in boys. I set aside the moral versus immoral debate going inside my cerebrum. Sometimes thinking less is better. Keep things simple and you will be happy. I pulled her towards myself. Surprisingly she pushed me back to recline on the sofa. We allowed our tongues to play vigorously. I felt Bharti's hands on the hottest part of my body. Girls like it very much though they hesitate admitting it. I slipped my hand inside her shirt. The sofa was getting hotter than ever. Suddenly something happened to me. I closed my mouth, removed my hands from her breasts and gave a gentle push to her.

"I think we should stop," fear of guilt inside me spoke.

Bharti looked at me with disappointment. Nobody wants to have incomplete romance. It makes one more desperate and pissed off. "Goodnight," I hurried back to my room. I tried to shut up my brain but it kept harping on. One of the judges on the show remarked that Bharti and I were a charismatic pair. We had something called the 'X-factor'. We really had it. That is why we survived so many eliminations to reach the top two. The only ones left were Tina and Yash.

Had they also done what I and Bharti tried to do today? Maybe she was besotted with me. Thoughts kept flooding my mind. What's if I had not stopped? "What's immoral? Stupid." Naidu's words flashed in my mind.

Joker's Jottings

Start learning yoga! It helps with you-know-what? Never write true things about your life in a diary. Diary is a land of secrets that always brings trouble!

Never say a 'no' to a girl. I missed a chance with Bharti, my voluptuous mate. I forgot that nothing is immoral until your girl finds out. Love libido. Believe me, it is better than fingers and shakes. Quite!

Chapter Fourteen

The Grand Finale & The Goodbye

Next day, all the three judges came to the hotel to wish us. It was a big day for all of us. The tension was at its peak. My parents were on a tour of Varanasi, offering prayers in the temples for my success. I love the word 'family'. It is the best thing about being an Indian. We were to leave for shooting location at 5:30 p.m. At ten past five my preparations for the finale were disturbed by a knock on the door. As I opened the door, I was dumbfounded to see the person standing there.

"You!"

Aditi was standing there. No doubt, she was looking gorgeous as ever. I was very elated to see her but she did not

reciprocate the same excitement and joy.

"Come inside," I said in an excitement.

Aditi had got admission in a reputed college of Delhi University. She had taken all the pain to come so far, just to meet me. It was a pleasant surprise for me.

"You can't imagine how happy I am," the smile on my face kept being wider.

Her face continued to be stiff.

"I know you are angry with me. Believe me, there is a misunderstanding between us. Bharti and I are just friends. No romance or relationship."

"You don't need to explain that," she finally spoke. She was boorish in her tone.

"Then why are you behaving so strange? You don't know how much I missed you."

"I know everything."

"What?"

"That you did."

"What did I do?" Did she come to know about what happened last night between me and Bharti? Nay, that is impossible, I thought.

"I never expected this from you. Riya told me everything that you and Naidu did that night at Delhi."

I almost got paralysed. She was talking about the one night stand I had with that sex worker. My lips did not move.

I had asked Naidu to keep it a secret, but he must have told Vivek, who spilled out in front of Riya. There was no other possibility by which Aditi could have come to know about all that. How could they be so careless and stupid? Slapdash Turds, I cursed.

"I am really sorry. It happened impulsively. Please forgive me," I mustered courage to plead.

"You know what? I don't even want to see your face. You deserve nothing but…"

Slap. Slap. Slap. Three in a row!

"The day I came to know about this, I decided to end our relationship. You brutally raped my trust. I was a fool to have blind faith in you."

"Please don't say so. Please," I whined.

"And for your kind information, I am seeing a senior in my college. He loves me a lot. And we have even done; anyway leave it."

"What!" I felt the pangs of guilt and jealousy simultaneously. I loved Aditi and she cannot be anybody else's.

"You taught me a bitter lesson. I brought this bag for you. It contains all your lies. Cards, letters, gifts, everything you gave me. And please do not try to contact me. Our relationship is over."

She dropped the bag on the bed. "Please Aditi. Give me a chance. I can prove my unconditional love for you. Even you know that we are made for each other."

"Stop. Don't even think so," her heart had turned into a stone. Emotionless and impervious!

"Can you live without me?"

"Yes. That is exactly I have been doing for the last few months. You are nowhere in my life. Don't even think that your tears can make me change my mind."

She walked towards the door. I felt somebody wringing my heart.

"All the luck for your grand finale," she slammed the door hard and walked away. Aditi walked out of my life. Forever! I knelt down and kept crying. Love and then loss! The circle completed. One mistake robbed everything from my life. I felt like I had lost my eyesight. It was all dark. I started knocking the floor with my fists. Harder and harder! But it didn't hurt. Aditi left me numb. A broken heart is too hard to bear.

All the while, I kept muttering "Aditi, I love you. Don't leave me. Please." But she was too far away to have heard this. The floor got stains of my blood and tears. Darkness filled my soul. The joy of being in the grand finale of such a big TV show was miles and miles away.

The phone's ring made a cross-over tone with my sighs. I stopped mine and picked it up.

"Ready?" Vineet sir on the other side asked.

"Yes," I said. I tried to be normal.

"Are you okay?" he figured out the abnormality in my tone.

"Yeah, I am fine," I lied. I was back to the nadir of despair.

"Come downstairs. Your beauticians are waiting in the caravan."

"Okay." It was really a very hard situation for me. On one side, I lost my love and on other side, I needed to compete in a finale. Not only mine but Bharti's dream was also connected to that. I washed my face and hands and came down to the caravan.

Cosmetics can hide wrinkles and pimples but they cannot hide pain and agony. I was broken and in a state where there was a complete incompleteness. I did not want to participate in the grand finale. But running away is not always an option.

The grand finale was scheduled to start at 7 p.m. The stage was set at the *ghats* of Varanasi. All the four contestants, jury members, show host and the crew members took their positions by 6:30 p.m. The stage looked magnificent. The *ghats* were basking in the river of colourful lights. The Ganga shone. An air of festivity wrapped the whole area. The local crowd turned out in huge numbers to witness the show. They shouted slogans and held placards. I saw that most of them were bearing my and Bharti's name. We were pitched as favourites. Three months of TV appearance gave me something which even the IIT-JEE topper does not get a place in the homes of lakhs of families. Everybody knew me well. They loved my dance. They voted for me. I had become a part of dining discussions, classroom gossips and news channels' sound bites. 'India's Musical Jodi' was a hit reality show. The best thing about a reality show is that it gives a platform for people who are passionate for fame and art. Unfortunately, the sad part is that it sells their aspirations in the process. The grand finale went on air at the scheduled time. Lakhs of people were anxious for the result.

"Voting lines were closed yesterday only. The counting has been also done. I hope it is us," Bharti said. I did not reply. I was not in a mood.

She further continued, "But I fear that Tina might use her political links to clinch the title," I still kept mum. Tina's maternal uncle was an M.P and an influential politico. He did visit our sets a couple of times and shared a very healthy relationship with the director and the producer of the show. We Indians are good at both—abusing politicians as well as licking their feet. Being ambiguous is pragmatic! Some of the fellow contestants had even alluded to clown-in-*kurta* M.P's involvement in manipulating things. Reality is never devoid of politics, so how could a reality show be an exception?

"Are you upset with what happened last night?" Bharti asked.

"No. it is okay. I am fine," I had almost forgotten what happened last night. The bigger always swallows the smaller. At that time I was in a bigger fix.

"I was serious last night and I meant what I did. I find you attractive and suave."

"Let us talk about it later. Its finale and we should focus on it," I tried to divert the discussion.

"Okay! It's cool. Then let's rock the stage tonight. We should do it the winners' way," she was very energetic in her tone. I nodded. After all, I too had great plans to make the finale a fascinating extravaganza. But how could a broken heart dance?

The chain of performances came to an end after two hours. With every sizzling performance, the crowd became hysteric. Finally, it was result time. All four of us stood at the centre of the stage. The chief guest was a famous Bollywood biggie. He along with the judges was asked to come on the stage.

The host broke the silence. "Our journey to search India's Musical Jodi has come to an end. For the last hundred days, you and we have stayed together. The success of this show is attributed to your love. I would like to disclose that our contestants have received more than 20 million votes. Twenty million votes! That is how enormous your love for them is."

The crowd clapped. He continued further. "Out of these two pairs, one pair will become India's first Musical Jodi. But which pair will be that? Even I don't know. Actually the picture is slightly different. A little strange! We were in a fix after compilation of the results. I know you must be wondering why I am saying so. In the next two minutes everything will be clear. Watch this video to discover the mystery."

A visual appeared on the big screen. All eyes glued to that. The only ray of hope in my life started flickering. There was a tie. Out of four zones, we led in north and west and the other two were won by Tina and Yash. It was a 2-2.

"What if Tina's uncle influenced the judges?" Bharti whispered in my ears. The callousness of showbiz world made nothing impossible. No ethics, only tactics. That is the *mantra*.

"Maybe everything is being framed to make them the winner," I missed having no links in politics.

"I am really agitated. I don't want to lose. The title is everything for me."

"I know. Keep calm. Lets us wait for the final decision," I consoled her.

All the jury members went backstage to discuss the next step. The final decision rested in their hands. Ten minutes later, they returned with smiles on their faces. Playing God is always a pleasure. One of the juries took the mike.

"We were surprised as we didn't expect a tie. After a very serious discussion, we have decided to conduct a secret voting amongst all the other eliminated contestants of this show. The pair with the maximum number of votes wins the title."

The decision of the jury members was unconventional. Weirdo! All the eliminated eight pairs who were part of the show went backstage for the secret voting.

From the very beginning of the show, Bharti and I were projected as the strongest contender. The juries' boundless appreciation made us an eyesore for others. Still we survived. We knew the other pairs were jealous of us and the judges had given them an opportunity to take a sweet revenge.

"This is not fair. Our popularity may backfire. These people never liked us," Bharti remarked. On the one hand, the long wait was killing us and on the other hand, fear of being victimised was stalking us.

"Just pray and have faith. Nothing is in our hands." There was nothing better I could have said. Tension, tension and tension! It was all around. We felt smothered. Being part of suspense is vulnerable.

The drama took 30 minutes to conclude. The host returned to the stage with an envelope. There was a mysterious smile on his face.

"I know that you guys are waiting anxiously to know the results. Thanks for being such a nice audience. I would also like to thank all our sponsors for their immense support. I won't keep the suspense any longer. The winner's name is written in this sealed envelope," he announced and gave a wide grin. He looked at us and his grin became wider.

"Without any delay, I am going to open it," he opened the envelope, smiled and continued, "Well, the winner has got five votes out of eight. And the winner is...the winner is..."

"*Om namah shivay, Om namah shivay, Om namah shivay,*" Bharti kept muttering the *mantra*. Our hearts ran like horses. Alas! My horse was injured.

"....the pair which is India's first Musical Jodi is....is....Abhi and Bharti....."

"Hip hip hurray..." Bharti screamed and jumped into the air. The whole crowd applauded us. Firecrackers covered the sky. I felt good but not happy. An absolute razzmatazz followed the announcement.

"So I would request our chief guest, Mr Khan, to crown the winners and hand over a cheque of 25 lakh rupees. Besides this, they have won a contract of the video album with M4U TV. A big round of applause for Abhi and Bharti.....India's first Musical Jodi," the host announced.

Tina and Yash congratulated us. Their hearts broke too,

but their agony was lesser than mine. The chief guest crowned me and said. "Congratulations, son. This is a king's crown. Go and rule the world."

I looked at the VIP lobby near the stage. Papa and Maa were waving at me. They were happy that their son had finally achieved something. Their prayers yielded.

Should I ask them to undertake one more tour of the temples? For Aditi, I thought.

"So, Abhi, how are you feeling after this win?" the host handed over the mike to me.

"Thank you all for making this happen. An individual never wins. It is always a team's effort that makes it possible. In our case it was me, Bharti, our parents, our friends and you all who made this possible. But today I want to say something, something that turned my whole world topsy-turvy," I choked. Tears rolled down my cheeks. Certainly they weren't of happiness. I wiped them off and resumed, "Today I lost something, somebody I loved, someone who loved me. I made a mistake and now she is gone. Losing her is like putting flowers on my own grave. Mr Khan just now said that this is a prince's crown." I pointed towards the coronet on my head and continued, "But I feel that fate has rewarded me with the joker's crown. I fear going in front of the mirror with this crown for the mirror will laugh at me. Treasureless-trove a man is without love. I cheated her and now fate has made a joke out of me. Anyway, I have won and I am thankful to all of you. I should put on the mask and act happy."

I took the joker's crown off my head. I kissed it and smiled. The whole world watched it. I still had Bharti's proposal open. Can we really make a great pair? Who knows? Thoughts invaded me. The mask was on. Love, live and lose. The circle never stops.

That night I made an entry in my diary.

Love is a song, sing it.

Open your arms and embrace it.

Wherever you go, whatever you do

Never close your eyes for love can fly.

It is pure, it's gentle, and it's eternal.

It is everywhere and it can be nowhere.

For me love was nowhere. At least for that moment! Unfulfilment is also one facet of love.

Joker's Jottings

You need a heart to love, not a girl. I have a loaded one. Hey sexy girls out there! Are you listening?

The Saga of Love via Telephone

By Pankaj Pandey

Price : Rs. 99
Pages : 104
Size : 5.5×8.5 inches
Binding : Paperback
Language : English
Subject : Fiction/Romance
ISBN : 9788183520669

About the book:

Love means never losing hope...

He is Pankaj, a creative and innovative guy of an engineering college.

She is Shikha, a sensation. Her voice is that of a nightingale.

They fall in love without an eye-contact talk, share everything, foresee future...

Destiny had something in their fate...

This novel takes you to a journey of love, romance, passion, thrill and saturnine events.

About the Author:

Pankaj Pandey, a technocrat turned writer, is an ex-student of Babu Banarsi Das Institute of Technology, Ghaziabad. He is an eloquent speaker and is striving to be successful in the field of leadership, life improvement and consultancy.

Media Reviews:

The Saga of Love is a vibrant and cherished love story. *Organiser*

A unique love story via the telephonic conversation which is beautifully written by the author. *Dainik Jagran*

She turned, I saw her turning

By Mushtaq Ahmad & Nabi Nazeer

Price	:	Rs. 99
Pages	:	112
Size	:	5.0×7.75 inches
Binding	:	Paperback
Language	:	English
Subject	:	Fiction/Romance
ISBN	:	9788183520690

About the book:

Musmad, an orphan, spends his life wandering over hills and sitting near the riverside when, one day, his eyes fall on Fairynelo. She, however, is unaware of his affection and gets married to Iranzir. When Musmad sees her leaving her parental home in the car with her husband Iranzir, Musmad, completely heartbroken, runs after the car for some distance and then drops on the ground, wailing, *She turned; I saw her turning.*

All of a sudden, the story takes a new twist, causing an upheaval in the lives of the key protagonists. New characters emerge on the scene, while the constant refrain in this tragic tale depicting the pain of unrequited love is *She turned. I saw her turning.*

GOLDEN CLASSICS

Complete & Unabridged Editions

****

Antoine de Saint-Exupéry | The Little Prince | 112 pp | Rs. 69

Charles & Mary Lamb | Tales from Shakespeare | 320 pp | Rs. 99

George Orwell | 1984 | 328 pp | Rs. 149

George Orwell | Animal Farm | 128 pp | Rs. 95

Hermann Hesse | Siddhartha | 168 pp | Rs. 119

Jane Austen | Sense & Sensibility | 320 pp | Rs. 99

Kahlil Gibran | The Prophet | 112 pp | Rs. 69

Kahlil Gibran | The Broken Wings | 120 pp | Rs. 60

Kahlil Gibran | A Tear and a Smile | 160 pp | Rs. 69

Lewis Carroll | Alice in Wonderland | 128 pp | Rs. 60

Maxim Gorky | Mother | 400 pp | Rs. 175

Rabindranath Tagore | Gitanjali | 128 pp | Rs. 60

Robert Louis Stevenson | Treasure Island | 224 pp | Rs. 70

Rudyard Kipling | The Jungle Book | 192 pp | Rs. 70

Rudyard Kipling | Tales from India | 320 pp | Rs. 149

Rudyard Kipling | Kim | 312 pp | Rs. 149

William Shakespeare | Romeo and Juliet | 128 pp | Rs. 60

William Shakespeare | Macbeth | 128 pp | Rs. 60